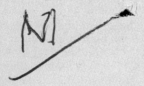

Love without marriage was, to Judy, a desert of emotional insecurity. She promised Malcolm Stewart a lifetime of loving and he turned her down. They loved one another, but saw their future together differently. Judy couldn't just live with Malcolm ... but she couldn't live without him, either.

THE IMPOSSIBLE WOMAN

BY
EMMA DARCY

MILLS & BOON LIMITED
15–16 BROOK'S MEWS
LONDON W1A 1DR

*First published in Great Britain 1985
by Mills & Boon Limited*

© Emma Darcy 1985

*Australian copyright 1985
Philippine copyright 1986
This edition 1986*

ISBN 0 263 75256 9

*Set in Monophoto Plantin 11 on 11 pt.
05-0286 – 49075*

*Made and printed in Great Britain by
Richard Clay (The Chaucer Press) Ltd,
Bungay, Suffolk*

CHAPTER ONE

JUDY grimaced in disgust. No imagination anywhere! Her gaze swept from side to side as she drove slowly along but there was not one glimpse of originality in the landscaping. And this was the highly touted Executive Estate—*the* place to live on the edge of Gosford City, complete with heliport for convenient commuting to Sydney, just eighty kilometres away. The two and a half acre lots were in a prime position, close to the business heart of the Central Coast and only minutes away from some of the best beaches in the world. The houses which had been built were executive standard but the landscaping was conventional, middle-of-the-road.

Judy ached to put her knowledge and artistic flair to practical use. Common sense told her it took time to build a reputation as a landscape consultant. A ripple of depression whispered that establishing a reputation was well-nigh impossible with all the odds stacked against her.

The drawback of being young and female was difficult enough to overcome in a predominantly male field of work, but to be cute ... Judy winced. God! How she hated that word! It conjured up kewpie dolls, playful kittens, all kinds of frivolous, empty-headed things ... anything but a serious artist with expert knowledge of her craft. Knowledge and even solid, practical experience lost all weight when measured against her feminine cuteness.

5

Maybe if she had been a big, horsy woman, or a tall, proud Amazon—someone whose dignity of person commanded respect—but to be small and cute ... that was a combination which only inspired a sickening smile of male condescension. There was nothing she could do about her big blue eyes with their ridiculously long, curly lashes, and short of an operation, she could not make a straight nose out of a retroussé one. Her heart-shaped face with its 'cute' pointy chin could not be changed. She had grown her baby-blonde hair so that she could cram its curls into a bun or French roll, but even that had failed to lend her dignity. At just over five feet, she was too damned short!

Lot 27. Judy braked the truck to an abrupt halt. She had been so involved with her thoughts that she had almost missed the small signboard. Two larger signboards identifying architect and builder dwarfed the lot number into insignificance. Judy recognised the builder's name as one who specialised in quality homes, and quality it would have to be since the architect was Malcolm Stewart.

That name struck her with amazement. It was associated in her mind with large building complexes; shopping centres and skyscrapers, not private homes. His prize-winning design for a new tourist centre had been featured in a local newspaper some months ago. It would seem he had been persuaded into taking a small job while he was working in the area. His fee would have been prohibitive and Judy wondered if the owners were satisfied with his design or merely satisfied to boast that Malcolm Stewart had been their architect.

The view of the house from the road was certainly impressive. A high privacy wall extended from a central gateway to within ten metres of the side-boundaries. Huge, brick pillars served as sentinels to the wide opening and automatically drew the eye to the gabled roof of the house which peaked in line with the centre of the gateway. Three gables rose in beautiful symmetry like a soaring series of outstretched wings.

The lowest roof-line covered the front entrance to the house and provided a sheltered walkway from the car-ports or garages which were obviously situated behind the wall. The second line was the roof to the main body of the house. On either side of its peak rose an upright line of skylight windows which supported the highest gable. The visual impact was extraordinarily uplifting. Judy wondered if the interior matched up to the façade and was stirred by a lively curiosity to find out.

A dirt track ran up to the gateway and diverted to one side of the privacy wall, obviously giving access to the rear of the block by running down the boundary. The grounds at the front had been cleared of scrub but there had been no preparation done for lawn to be laid. The turf Judy was delivering could not be wanted here. She drove slowly, eyeing the house with keen interest. Once she had skirted the privacy wall the track dipped down and she saw that the house was split-level, the lower level forming a T-bar to the long central gable. Her fascination with the design was abruptly broken by the sight of a man waving her to a halt.

Judy stopped the truck and watched the man's

approach. He had the kind of physique which was very watchable. The glisten of sweat gave a golden sheen to a tanned body of rippling muscle. Ragged denim shorts hung loosely on lean hips and the man's only other concession to clothes was a battered straw hat. He was real pin-up material in any girl's book.

'Morning!' he called good-naturedly and his voice had a pleasant depth to it.

'It's a hot one,' Judy replied as she climbed out of the driver's cab and dropped to the ground.

He pulled up short and tipped his hat back, eyeing her with startled surprise. 'Thought it was the turf arriving.'

'It is the turf arriving,' Judy confirmed drily. 'Where do you want it set down?'

He took off his hat and ruffled his hair. It was straight and centre-parted, its thickness cut into layers to shape around his ears. 'Well, I'll be damned!' he muttered and his mouth widened to a grin of flashing white teeth. 'I wasn't expecting Daisy Mae to deliver it.'

'Daisy Mae?' Judy quizzed, not quite sure if she should feel affronted or not.

He chuckled and it was a pleasant, friendly sound. 'I guess my age is showing. The comic strip of *Li'l Abner* stopped some years ago but you sure are a dead-ringer for Daisy Mae. Black shorts, spotted shirt, big blue eyes, blonde pigtails and a traffic-stopping figure.'

Judy sighed. 'Look, mister! I'm glad I've given you your little joke for the morning, but if you'll just show me where you're going to lay the turf, I'll get on with my job and you can get on with yours. Okay?'

He shrugged and his grin turned lop-sided. 'Didn't mean to give offence but you are kind of little to be doing men's work.'

'Yeah ... and cute,' Judy drawled in exasperation. 'I know it's hard for a big he-man like yourself to believe that I'm capable of lifting anything more than a tea-towel, but do please lead on.'

Her jibe did not dim his good humour. In fact his eyebrows jiggled waggishly and his rather startling green eyes danced at her as he swept out an arm in exaggerated invitation. 'I await your pleasure, dear lady. An inspection of the site will be carried out forthwith.'

Judy could not help laughing. His humour was contagious. 'Who are you? The gardener?' she asked curiously.

'Ummmh ...' He slanted her a twinkling look as she fell into step beside him. 'More like a resident labourer. Sort of a caretaker-handyman. What's your name?'

'Judy. Judy Campbell. What's yours?'

'I can't resist it. You'll have to call me Punch.'

Judy burst out laughing again. 'Did anyone ever tell you you're mad?'

'Not as mad as a girl like you delivering turf,' he retorted lightly, then held up a hand to stop her protest. 'Say no more. I know you're going to make me eat my words and probably a few earthworms as I grovel in the dirt at your feet. In fact I'm almost convinced you're really Mrs Muscles Universe in disguise.'

'Not quite,' Judy conceded with an amused grin. 'But I manage all right.'

A potted tree was sitting on the edge of the track, beside it a freshly dug hole. Clearly the tree was destined for the hole. Judy stopped walking and shook her head in disgust. 'Did the owner tell you to plant that tree there?'

The man struck a semi-belligerent pose, folding his arms while he considered the tree, the hole and her air of lofty contempt. 'What's wrong with there?'

Judy folded her arms and rolled her eyes skywards. 'Oh, just about everything. But don't let me stop you. I'm just delivering turf.' She dropped her voice to a mournful tone. 'Poor tree! Hasn't got a hope of survival.'

The man stroked his chin and pursed his lips. 'Well now, I'd be the last person to condemn a tree to unnecessary death. I don't suppose a turf-deliverer like yourself would know where this tree might enjoy a long and healthy life?' One eyebrow slanted upwards as did one corner of his mouth. 'I lost the label.'

His wry admission brought a smile to her lips. 'It's an *Acer palmatum*. Japanese Maple in layman's language.'

'Ah!' Again he stroked his chin as if giving the matter grave consideration but the green eyes held a provocative tease. 'Could a humble labourer beg some expert advice?'

'Maybe,' she teased back. 'But right now I've got a job to do. I'll take a look around later.' And maybe he would show her through the house, a favour for a favour so to speak.

They continued walking. A wide sandstone terrace swept along the rear of the house and a swimming-pool was set off the far end of it. In line with the central gable of the house was a wide set of sandstone steps which led down to an all-weather tennis court. The slope on either side of the steps had been dug up and raked over in preparation for instant lawn.

'I want half the turf dumped here so I can wheelbarrow it along the terrace to the other side of the steps, and the rest spaced down the slope on this side. Can do?' the man asked matter-of-factly.

'No problem,' Judy mumbled, her gaze taking in the fantastic wall of tinted glass which rose to the gabled peak on this northern side of the house. It was broken only by a series of brick pillars which supported the roof. These were spaced with perfect symmetry, one on each corner and one on either side of the gable where it dipped to join the wings. Not only was the design impressive but the wall of glass would capture the winter sun and give a marvellous sense of space, almost bringing the outdoors inside.

'Like it?'

Judy glanced up at the man who was regarding her with amused interest. 'Are you going to be the window-cleaner?'

He laughed and shook his head.

'The trouble with architects,' Judy continued in dry comment, 'is that they make everything look good, but they don't give too much thought to practical living, like housework and being able to keep the place tidy. But I guess the owners can afford help. I'll go and bring the truck down.'

She was even more curious now to see inside the house. Malcolm Stewart was renowned for his clever and artistic use of glass but she wanted to see just how good he was when it came to fulfilling the demands of a truly liveable house. Surely she could persuade the man to show her through. Sometimes it was quite useful to be female and reasonably attractive, Judy decided, then mocked herself for being so two-faced about her appearance.

All the same, she felt pleased that the man liked her. She liked him. His zany humou. amused her and he was obviously good-natured, easy-going, and very, very good-looking. His face was unusual, striking rather than handsome. Those broad, high cheekbones, the strong nose and wide, full-lipped mouth somehow reminded her of American Indians. The coppery hair and bronzed skin emphasised the impression. She did not wonder that he was a casual labourer. He even looked like a carefree nomad, taking life as it came, breezily confident that something would always turn up for him.

She climbed into the truck, released the brake and let it roll down the slope until it was in position for the first set-down near the terrace. By the time she had released the side and back boards the man had reappeared with a wheelbarrow.

'Might as well lift some rolls straight on to the barrow,' he said, reaching out to gather one off the truck.

Judy smiled. If he was intent on helping her she was not about to refuse. With each roll consisting of a two-metre length of turf some thirty centimetres wide, unloading was heavy work. 'If you have an old, long-sleeved shirt handy, I'd suggest you put it on,' she advised as she rolled down her own sleeves and buttoned them at the wrist. She was conscious of his gaze on her but proceeded to undo the knot at her midriff and pull her shirt down to hang loosely over her hips.

'And if I don't have a shirt handy?'

She threw him a knowing grin as she reached into the truck for her gardening gloves. 'You'll get a mass of irritating scratches on your arms and stomach. The grass roots can be pretty mean on your skin. Please yourself, but don't say I didn't warn you.'

'You do this for a living?'

The puzzled, slightly incredulous note in his voice made her grin even wider. 'It's the outdoors life. I love it.'

He went off shaking his head. Judy could not repress a little giggle and spurred on by an urge to impress him, she swung straight into the task of unloading. There was a neat stack of rolls on the ground by the time he returned. He looked, frowned, then made short work of filling the wheelbarrow. His red-checked shirt had seen better days but it served to protect him.

'Don't you get a bad back from lifting these weights all the time?'

Judy threw him a teasing challenge. 'I'm very supple. Leave it to me if it's too much for you.'

'I was going to make the same offer,' he retorted drily, then trundled the barrow along the terrace.

He was back almost immediately and Judy glanced around in puzzled surprise. He had set the rolls down without stopping to spread them across the prepared earth. 'They'll dry out if you leave them and you're making double work for yourself, having to lift them twice. Better to drop them straight into position as you take them off the barrow . . . if you don't mind my telling you,' she added hastily, conscious of having sounded bossy. Men didn't like being told what to do and he was being very chivalrous about saving her work.

'I never argue with an expert,' he declared good-humouredly. He watched the steady rhythm of her action for a few moments before reloading his barrow. 'You really do do this for a living?'

'Not exactly. Our regular delivery man is off sick today so I'm filling in.'

'Is selling turf a good business?'

'Not a bad sideline. The pot plants do best and cut flowers have a good market. My speciality is landscaping but business is hard to come by.'

'Hence the tree knowledge.'

'Uh-huh. Not much I don't know about trees, particularly eucalypts.' She straightened and gave him a wry smile. 'Trouble is . . . my Daisy Mae image doesn't help in getting anyone to take me seriously.'

His eyes ran up her shapely legs and lingered on the thrust of nicely rounded breasts. 'Yeah . . . well, I'd have to say it's a distraction.' His gaze lifted to hers and the green eyes danced mischief. 'But me—I like to have that kind of distraction around any time, work or play. You know, I wouldn't say cute . . . more cuddly.'

He was off with the barrow before Judy could come up with a retort. She watched him go the length of the terrace. He had a cheeky bottom and fantastic legs. She wished she could think of some similarly provocative remark but the only word which came to mind was sexy. He was certainly that with his wicked green eyes.

He grinned at her as he rolled out the first strip of ready-made lawn. 'Am I doing it right?'

'You could hardly go wrong,' she replied shortly and returned to work, a little flustered at having been caught staring. She did not usually stare at men, appraising them in such a physical way.

'Isn't there another man at the nursery who could've done this?' he asked when he came for another load.

'Dad's got a bad heart and Billy's cutting and rolling the next load,' she explained matter-of-factly.

'Who's Billy?'

'My brother.'

A grim smile curved her mouth downwards. She wondered how this man would have reacted to her brother if Billy had come with her. Most people shied away, either discomfited by his childlike manner or imagining that retarded meant dangerous. At nineteen, Billy had the body of a man but his mind had not progressed beyond that of the eight-year-old he had been when struck down by meningitis.

'No boyfriend to help?'

She looked up to meet frankly speculative eyes. 'No boyfriend,' she stated flatly.

'Amazing!' he declared and trundled off again.

Judy sighed. Boyfriends! She had not had a serious boyfriend since David, and that had only been serious on her side, not on his. Certainly not on his. She had been incredibly naïve over David Barker but she had only been nineteen then, a country girl new to the big city life of Sydney. Having been brought up to believe she was as good as anybody else, it had not occurred to her that she was not 'good enough to marry'.

She had been well and truly smitten by David's dark good looks and experienced charm. He had romanced her in lavish fashion. Only in hindsight had Judy realised that he had been amused by her wide-eyed reaction to sophisticated city entertainment. She remembered how bored and uncharacteristically ill-at-ease he had been at her home on the one visit she had persuaded him into. He had somehow made her feel ashamed of having a brother like Billy, but she had been too blindly infatuated to take that as a warning sign of his true character.

When he had in turn asked her home for a weekend Judy had been delighted, anticipating an introduction to his family. Her mouth now twisted into a grimace as she recalled her awe at seeing the Barker home, a two-storeyed mansion in Turramurra, one of Sydney's class suburbs. Her sudden attack of nerves had been quite unnecessary. The Barkers had been away on holiday and David's idea of a weekend at his home had not been Judy's. She would never forget his derisive laughter when she had innocently spoken of 'waiting for marriage'.

She had been very abruptly disillusioned. In a very charming way, of course. But what it came down to was a different social rating. Little country bumpkins, although very sweet and bedworthy, simply did not rate as potential marriage partners. It had been a very hurtful and humiliating thump down to earth.

Over the last three years Judy had enjoyed other men's company from time to time but had felt no strong attraction to anyone. She had sometimes wondered if David had killed any spontaneity of feeling for the opposite sex but now she knew it was not so. Here she was fancying a man quite madly. He was fun. And she found him very, very attractive. She wondered if he would like a job in the nursery. Her father had been talking of hiring another hand.

'Is this a permanent job you've got here?' she asked when he returned for another load.

'I'll stay as long as it's convenient,' he asnwered vaguely. 'I like it here. Nice place.'

'That's something of an understatement. The house alone must have cost a fortune with Malcolm Stewart as its architect.'

'Do I detect a note of disapproval?'

She threw him a smile. 'Envy probably. Was he worth the fee?'

'What do you think?'

She shrugged. 'The shell looks great, but as I said before, some architects get so wrapped up in their special effects they lose sight of the fact that a house is for living in.'

'Oh, I reckon I could live in it very comfortably,' he drawled, amusement rippling through his voice. 'But then I'm not a family man. Have you seen any of his work?'

'Only his public stuff. I didn't know he did private homes.'

'Some. Or so I understand,' he added quickly.

'You've met him then?'

'On the job, so to speak.'

'What's he like?'

'I'd say he's a guy who likes to get his own way.'

His amusement was so pronounced Judy was prompted to ask, 'What's so funny?'

He laughed and shook his head. 'You keep surprising me. Why do you want to know what Malcolm Stewart's like?'

'Well, you'd think he'd care enough about his creation to insist on proper landscaping,' she declared with feeling. 'I mean, all that beautiful symmetry deserves to be highlighted, and here you are, pottering around, planting trees in the wrong places . . .'

'Only one tree. And that was an unrequested gift which had to planted to please the donor.'

Judy threw up her hands in disgust. 'That's right! Anything goes in the garden! I bet Malcolm Stewart wouldn't have put a glob of stained glass into that gable just because someone had given it to him.'

He grinned. 'You could be right.' He cocked his head to one side and his expression became more speculative. 'What about this lawn? Is it a mistake?'

She sighed and cast her eye over the area. 'No. You couldn't do anything else but grass this slope. Gardens would detract from the impact of the glass gable. And no doubt the owner wants a clear view of the tennis court.'

'I'm relieved that it has your approval. I'd hate to have to undo this work.'

She gave a self-derisive laugh. 'Who'd take any notice of what I said?'

'I would,' he declared emphatically and took off with another barrow-load.

He left her smiling. He really was a nice man. At least he made her feel good. She climbed back into the truck and gave him a cheery wave. 'Just going to turn around.' His exaggerated salute made her laugh.

She reversed up the track, made a neat turn, then slowly and carefully reversed down so that the remaining turf could be unloaded with economy of movement. Despite her hints the man had not offered to show her the interior of the house. However, there was still plenty of time and she could always bargain with the tree or try a few feminine wiles. He was attracted to her. And sex appeal had to be good for something. Except she didn't want him getting any wrong ideas.

On the other hand, maybe it was time she had some wrong ideas herself. Here she was, twenty-two years old, and still a virgin, waiting for some mythical man to marry. The truth was, she had never really been tempted to make love with any man, not even David. He had been more of a romantic figure than a sexual one. It was rather curious and disconcerting to suddenly feel a physical chemistry she had never felt before.

She climbed out of the truck and eyed her fellow worker speculatively as he pushed the wheelbarrow back again. 'I can't call you Punch,' she declared, wanting to be told his real name.

'Why not? What's in a name, as Romeo said. Or was it Juliet? You'd make a great Juliet with that lovely fresh skin and youthful glow.'

She flushed at his frank admiration. 'I'm not fourteen, you know.'

His eyebrows shot up. 'I should hope not. That sexy body of yours would tempt any man into carnal knowledge.'

Her face burnt. 'Really!'

He grinned at the feeble protest. 'All that bending over in short shorts is getting to me. Not to mention the way your shirt is clinging to more obtrusive parts. Luckily I am a master of self-control so have no fear, fair Judy. My appreciation of your beauty will remain strictly visual.'

He made it impossible to take offence. 'I suppose that's a compliment,' Judy mocked.

'Of course. And what's more, I find myself very grateful to the delivery man who's off sick. I didn't expect to enjoy this morning quite so much.'

It was all very well to be appreciated but Judy found that she was terribly conscious of her body from that moment on, conscious of her shorts riding up, conscious of her shirt sticking to her and very conscious of a green-eyed gaze. At last there were only the rolls down the centre of the truck to be unloaded. The man suggested that she climb up and hand the turf down to him. Judy flatly refused to be put so much under his disturbing gaze and insisted that he climb up if he was intent on helping.

'Now I can admire your legs,' she taunted when he finally agreed to the arrangement.

'You're welcome to admire all of me,' he retorted wickedly. 'Which gives me a splendid idea. Bring your bikini with you when you return with the next load. We'll have a well-earned swim in the pool. Nothing like a bit of relaxation after a good day's work.'

She only hesitated for a moment. It might be living dangerously but ... why not? 'Okay! You're on,' she said recklessly, and then wished she hadn't quite expressed herself in those exact words.

The answering gleam in those suggestive green eyes was clear enough warning that his visual appreciation might turn very physical, and Judy's heart performed several agitated little flips. She told herself she was quite mad to flirt with the idea of an involvement with a man who was obviously a carefree drifter, but she had never been so tempted in her life.

Besides, it was only a swim. No big deal. She could always back off later. She could control the situation any way she liked. She always had before. No problem. It wouldn't hurt to swim with the tide a little way.

CHAPTER TWO

THE truck was loaded, ready to go again. Judy was impatient to be on her way but common sense insisted that she eat a good lunch. The morning's work had made her hungry and there would be no less work this afternoon. She could not afford to get faint on the job, not when she had made so many claims of capability.

'Want Billy to go with you this afternoon?'

Judy glanced up at her father and shook her her head. 'No thanks, Dad. I can handle it.'

'I'll help you, Sis. I like going in the truck.'

She smiled across at her brother whose mouth was poised to bite into the huge dagwood sandwich he had made of his salad. 'Thanks, Billy, but not today.' Her gaze swung back to her father. 'Actually the man I'm delivering to helped unload the truck this morning and I'm sure he'll lend a hand again so it's not so much of a chore.'

'Uh-huh.' Drew Campbell's slow smile had a sly twist. 'Find some advantages in being a woman, did you?'

Her answering grin was an admission. 'Well I'm off now. Thanks for lunch, Mum.'

Tess Campbell showed her surprise. 'Don't you want a cup of tea? What's the hurry?'

'Too hot for tea. I think I'll go for a swim after work so don't worry if I'm late getting home.'

Judy was out of the kitchen before any more questions could be asked, like where and with whom and for how long. The problem in living with parents was that they always wanted to know everything. Judy smiled to herself as she dashed into the bedroom for beach-towel and bikini. She didn't have any answers, not even the man's name. Punch. In a funny kind of way it suited him and it was obvious that names carried little weight as far as he was concerned. He had certainly not been in any awe of Malcolm Stewart. Judy decided she liked that.

The fizz of anticipation was in her driving. The truck zoomed down hills and zipped through corners on a line which would have done a racing driver proud. Judy's gaze did not wander from the road. Her interest in landscaping had been crowded out by a steady flow of speculative thoughts which focused entirely on the man.

He was a good few years older than her. Thirtyish, she imagined. The laughter lines around his eyes were too well entrenched for him to be younger than that and he had the comfortable self-assurance which comes with experience. These days there was a growing number of people dropping out of the competitive rat-race of society, seeking alternative life-styles. Judy, herself, did not relish the thought of a nine-to-five job in an office. Maybe he preferred to be his own man instead of pushing someone else's paper.

Then there were the people with itchy feet. Since jet planes and television had brought the world closer, many Australians were now travelling overseas whenever they could afford it, particularly the younger generation. Setting themselves into a job-career and tying themselves to families were goals which came later, if at all. Judy suspected that the man fell in this category.

He seemed the type who would ride future and fortune as it came, expecting both to smile on him. And they probably would. A man with his good looks and charm of manner would never be pushed behind a door. He was quite an individual.

One thing was certain. A relationship with him wouldn't run aground on social snobbery. Judy felt very comfortable with that thought although she had to smile at herself for fantasising so far. She had only met the man this morning and he had only asked her to have a swim with him.

Yet she felt . . . attuned to him? As if she could not help responding. It was curious, and exciting . . . and possibly risky. After all, she really knew nothing about him. Punch was an apt name. She was Punch-drunk to be thinking some of the things she had been thinking, not her normal self at all.

Her eyes automatically searched for him as she drove down the slope and parked beside the terrace. She could not see him. With a little sigh of disappointment she applied the hand-brake and switched off the ignition. Her hand hovered over the horn, tempted to announce her arrival.

'Hello again.'

Her head whipped around in surprise. He was rising from a sun-lounger near the pool, a smile of welcome on his face and only the briefest swimming-costume interrupting the nakedness of his superb body.

'I'll be right with you,' he called, bending to pick up his shorts and shirt from the terrace.

Unaccountably Judy's toes curled. She tore her gaze away from him, amazed at herself for being physically affected by the mere sight of a masculine body. It had never happened before. It made her feel like a giddy teenager reacting to a pop star. That's what comes from thinking about a man as a sexual object, she told herself sternly and took a deep breath to counteract her fluttering pulse.

'You'd better come and inspect my lawn-laying. Give it your stamp of approval,' he tossed at her as he proceeded to dress.

Judy climbed down from the truck and strolled along the terrace, making a deliberate effort to appear relaxed. Belatedly she noticed that all the turf had been transported to the other side of the steps. The rows of grass had been neatly jammed together and the instant lawn looked very smooth indeed.

'Great job! Better than most landscapers do,' she declared in a tone of authority.

'Nothing like the incentive of personal interest to do a job well.' He took the few steps which allowed him to rest a light hand on her shoulder while he swept the other arm over the results of his work. 'I had to impress you with this since I lost your respect over the tree.'

His proximity, the touch of his hand and the cheekiness of his grin sent a tingling warmth through Judy's body. He was impressing her all right. Too much too soon, for her peace of mind. 'Since you've completed this section, you'd do well to put a sprinkler on and give it a good soak. Keep it wet and cool,' she advised, and privately advised herself to keep cool too.

'At once, Fraulein Kommandant.'

She laughed as he saluted and moved off to do her bidding. The laughter held a hint of relief. She was considerably unnerved by her strong reaction to this man. While he positioned a sprinkler and turned it on she returned to the truck and released the side-boards.

'While I readily concede that you're the boss in these earthy matters,' he drawled provocatively as he joined her in releasing the back-board, 'I have given much thought to our work programme this afternoon.'

'You have?' Blue eyes mocked his assertion.

'Indeed I have,' he insisted gravely. 'It seems to me that it would be most desirable if we finish at the same time. Therefore I shall carry the rolls of turf to you while you spread it out with the same brilliant expertise I have already demonstrated. If, of course, you feel capable of matching my efforts.'

The challenge neatly covered the fact that he would be taking on the harder labour of lifting and carrying. Judy smiled at the deceit. 'If that's the way you want it, I'll do my level best.'

The green eyes danced at her in warm approval and for once, Judy did not mind a man taking charge and telling her what to do. They formed a very efficient team. As Judy finished setting each roll of turf another was positioned for her to continue the line. Neither of them spoke much except to offer a useful comment on the work in progress, but there was a very real sense of companionship between them. The afternoon sun was hot and Judy's shirt was sticking to her back by the time they were finished.

'Great job!' he declared, echoing her previous comment. 'Just goes to show how well we're matched.'

Judy's heart gave a delighted little skip. Then she chided herself for reading meanings where there were probably none. 'How's that?' she asked, wondering what he really thought of her.

'Look at that lawn! Both sides immaculate. You and I are a brilliant combination. Now there's only one task left to accomplish. Planting that troublesome little tree. Where should we dispose of it?'

'If I show you where to plant it, will you show me through the house?'

His eyes crinkled in amusement. 'Bargaining time, is it?'

Judy threw him a wide-eyed look of appeal. 'It wouldn't hurt to let me see, would it?'

He laughed and shook his head. 'I was going to invite you in anyway. I couldn't possibly miss hearing your critical opinion of Malcolm Stewart's work. Architects don't rate very highly according to some of the remarks you've made today. But first let's plant the tree and have our swim.'

Judy slanted him a wry look of exasperation. 'You knew all along that I wanted a look inside, didn't you?'

He grinned. 'I like things to progress in an orderly fashion. Work, then play.'

Apparently a tour of the house came under the heading of 'play' and his expression held a distinct gleam of 'Come into my parlour, said the spider to the fly'. Judy's pulse performed a little jig and she turned aside to cast her eye around the grounds.

There was no position which was not exposed to full sun and the *Acer palmatum* needed almost full shade to thrive in this climate. 'It's not the kind of tree I'd use with this house. Too ornamental,' she commented thoughtfully then gave a sigh of resignation. 'However, since it has to be planted, I'd suggest the south-east corner behind this wing of the house. That would give it the most shade, I think. It's a deciduous tree and if you put it on the other side, the leaves will get in the pool.'

'We certainly don't want leaves in the pool,' he declared emphatically. 'Come and supervise. You can point out the spot so I won't get it wrong again.'

The tree and mattock were promptly collected and another hole dug precisely where Judy indicated.

'Just out of interest, what trees would you plant in these grounds?' the man asked curiously as he bedded down the *Acer palmatum*.

Judy did not hesitate, having already envisaged what she would do, given the chance. 'Citriadoras out the front. Ironbarks and angophoras below the tennis court.'

He lifted his head and rolled his eyes at her. 'Like to elaborate on those technical terms?'

Judy grinned, enjoying the opportunity to show off her knowledge. 'Citriadoras are lemon-scented gum-trees. They have straight, tall trunks, very elegant, and their bark is almost white. The foliage is sparse but graceful, and wouldn't block the view of the house from the road. Ironbarks are also straight and very impressive with their rough, black bark, a contrast in texture and colour to the angophoras which are smooth and red with twisted limbs. An angophora lit by the setting sun is a fabulous sight.'

'You really do know your trees.'

The green eyes held a measure of respect and

Judy felt ridiculously pleased. 'I like Australian natives. They have a beauty all their own. I don't know why people always tend to choose English or American or Asian trees for their properties.'

'I guess because they're different. A garden instead of native bushland,' he said reasonably.

'Yeah, I guess so,' she agreed, grudging the truth of his statement. 'But take this house. It's been designed for the Australian climate. Why should the owners want to look out on foreign trees? It's stupid. But I bet they'll fill the place up with liquidambars and maples and all sorts of pine-trees. Just like everyone else.'

He stood up and brushed the dirt from his hands before placing them lightly on her shoulders. 'I wouldn't bet on that. However, you do look temptingly beautiful when you're all steamed up and I've been wanting to do this all day.'

Judy was caught open-mouthed. One hand slid up and tilted her chin and then his lips were on hers, a tantalising brush of sensation which tingled through her entire bloodstream. His other hand slid around the back of her neck and the kiss became a slow, sensuous exploration of her mouth, very deliberate, very thorough and intensely exciting. Her response was instinctive, a physical compulsion which had nothing whatsoever to do with thought processes. He did not move closer. There was no embrace, no body contact, just a kiss which was totally seductive in its promise of pleasures to come, a beginning which was a heady statement of mutual attraction.

He lightly stroked her cheek as he lifted his head away. The green eyes held a simmering warmth and the sensual mouth curved into a satisfied smile. A surge of heat swept into Judy's cheeks and a sharpened sense of self-preservation prompted her to dispel the electric intimacy.

'Playtime, huh?' she tripped out, pretending that the kiss had not affected her deeply.

His smile widened into a grin. 'Just about. There's a change-room at the back of the pool. You can get ready for our swim while I put the wheelbarrow and mattock away.' He touched her hot cheek with a teasing flick of his finger. 'I wouldn't want you to feel over-heated.'

'I have a built-in conditioner which automatically clicks on when the heat gets dangerous,' Judy declared airily, and walked away with a casual swing which denied anything but complete composure.

His soft laughter followed her. Judy's stomach curled a warning but she ignored it. The excitement tingling through her veins was too strong to deny. She fetched her towel and bikini from the truck and literally danced along the terrace, feeling delightfully alive and decidedly light-headed.

Set behind the line of the house was a cabana. Its central section was open to the pool and displayed a barbecue and snack-bar. To the left was a store-room for outdoors furniture and on the right a washroom comprising shower, toilet and vanity-bench. Every possible convenience had been provided and Judy decided that the owners had to be in the millionaire bracket. She wondered what it felt like to be so disgustingly rich and then smiled at the thought that she was about to enjoy the fruits of their wealth, a very private swimming-pool and the man they had employed.

He had stripped off his work-clothes and was at the refrigerator in the snack-bar when she emerged from the wash-room. The skimpiness of her yellow bikini had never troubled Judy. She was not fettered by inhibitions about her body and her well-rounded figure wore a bikini well. But one sweep of those green eyes stripped her naked and suddenly she felt uncomfortably vulnerable. Which was stupid. She was still in control of the situation. She could leave any time she liked. Get in the truck and go. He would not stop her.

'What do you fancy? Beer, coke, gin and tonic or vodka and orange?'

'A coke will do fine, thanks,' she answered lightly and strolled over to the edge of the pool

She sat down, dangling her legs in the water and telling herself there was no harm in the man. He was not the type to force himself on an unwilling woman. The only problem was in how willing he could make her feel ... and how willing she wanted to be.

He handed her an opened can of Coca-Cola and sat down next to her. 'Not going in yet?'

She sipped the coke without looking at him, all too sharply aware of the very masculine body beside her. Having slaked her thirst Judy concentrated on unwinding the rubber bands from her pigtails. 'I have to unbraid my hair first. It'll be a mass of knots if I don't.'

'I'll help you.'

He slid into the pool and with his body pressed against her leg, he began deftly separating the three thick swathes of hair from the pigtail closest

to him. Somehow Judy smothered a gasp and
kept her fingers working. She lowered her lashes
because his face was now on a direct level with
hers and she was not ready to meet those
knowing green eyes.

He raked through the released waves as if
fascinated by the silky texture. 'Lovely hair,
lovely body,' he murmured appreciatively.

She tossed the hair she had loosened over her
shoulder and looked at him with reckless
bravado. 'You rate pretty highly yourself. Nine
out of ten, I'd say,' she flung at him flippantly.

He grinned. 'I don't think I'll worry about the
missing point. You more than make up for it.'

His hands gripped her waist, lifting her with
effortless ease and before Judy could react one
way or another she was most definitely caught in
an embrace, and one which involved full body
contact, her feet floating helplessly around his
calves as he held her pinned against him.

'That's not fair,' she declared, thumping his
shoulders with the flat of her hands.

'No, but it feels great,' was his unabashed
retort. 'You have an incredibly tiny waist and the
curve of your spine is quite delicious. Not to
mention . . .' One hand had slid well below the
end of her spine.

'I'm warning you. If you say cute bottom I
shall sink my fangs into your throat.'

His grin grew more wicked. 'This bottom has
been teasing me all day. A very cheeky bottom.
The kind of bottom which begs to be . . .'

'So. You're a bottom man,' Judy mocked.

'I wouldn't say that. I could wax quite lyrical
about your breasts.' His gaze dropped to the soft
swell of flesh which her bikini-bra did little to hide.

'Why don't you dispense with the top? Then I can appreciate you to the full, so to speak.'

'Oh, a voyeur too, as well as a bottom man,' Judy cracked, pretending that his words had no effect on her and hoping that he could not hear the wild pounding of her heart.

'Totally depraved,' he murmured as his mouth came closer to hers and his eyes invited her to share all manner of depravity with him.

'Not so fast!' Judy's hand whipped up to prevent his mouth from wreaking havoc on her thinly held control. She forced a beguiling little smile. 'A swim in the pool, remember? A man as hot as you obviously needs cooling off. I wouldn't want you to get over-heated.'

He laughed at the mocking mimic of his own words. Then without any warning he plunged backwards into the water, dragging Judy with him and only releasing her when they were totally submerged. She struck swiftly away from him, needing a breathing space in more ways than one.

He wanted her, and the tricky part was he wanted her now, not next week or after a few dates. Judy was not used to such a direct, physical approach and although he excited her, the fact that he was being so blatantly physical gave her a creepy feeling. She did not want him to regard her as just another body for a pleasurable afternoon. And yet she could not help responding to him. And she wanted to respond to him.

Having lapped the pool several times in a steady crawl, Judy relaxed her body and floated on her back, enjoying the pleasant drift of water through her long hair. A head popped up beside her and a pair of green eyes twinkled their temptation.

'It's not working,' he stated decisively.

'What's not working?'

'The water. I don't feel the least bit cool with you lying there so provocatively. Come on out. We'll do the tour of the house.' He grabbed her hand and started dragging her towards the steps.

'We'll be dripping wet,' she protested at his hurry.

'I'll dry you off with a towel.'

'I can dry myself.'

'And deprive me of the pleasure of touching you? What a mean thought! Just when I was going to wrap you in a soft, cuddly towel.'

She frowned threateningly and he jiggled his eyebrows in appealing fashion so that she ended up laughing. He tossed the towel at her, not attempting to pursue the matter. Judy gave herself a brisk rub-down before attacking the wet thickness of her hair. By the time she finished a chaotic mass of damp ringlets framed her face and dangled around her shoulders. She looked up to see a wide, appreciative grin.

'Do you know you're an impossible woman? The body of a temptress and the head of an angel.'

'Well, just you concentrate on the head and we'll get on fine.'

He rolled his eyes upwards. 'She even asks the impossible. However . . .' he jangled a ring of keys at her and took firm possession of one of her hands, '. . . in the role of guide and show-master, I demand a certain amount of licence. Your hand is mine. Shall we follow the primrose path?'

'What primrose path?' she spluttered, unable to contain her amusement at his outrageousness even while shaking her head in weak reproach.

'Actually it's sandstone. We'll go up this side of the house so you can make the grand entrance through the front door.' He drew her along, pointing out features on the way. 'The kitchen and laundry are in this wing near the pool. Our path leads up to the garages to provide easy access for parcel-carrying if you don't want to go through the house. Here we have a clothes-line, neatly tucked out of sight behind the cabana but handy to the laundry-door. How am I doing so far?' he asked slyly.

'Ten out of ten.'

'Obviously my verbal skills outscore my physical attractions. I shall have to talk my way past your in-built conditioner.'

'You can verbal on all day,' she retorted happily, knowing she could cope with words.

'Now I understand why Punch hit Judy over the head,' he muttered darkly.

'Why?'

'It was the only way he could win.'

She threw him a haughty look of disdain. He chuckled and opened the gate to the front courtyard, inviting her through with an over-gallant sweep of the arm.

'Here we have garages on our right, car-ports for visitors on our left and a covered walkway from both areas converging on the entrance to the house.'

The courtyard itself had been gravelled but the walkway was sandstone and this continued up on to the front portico. The entrance doors were panelled cedar and their polished brass handles gleamed richly on the satin-finished wood. Judy tingled with anticipation as the doors were unlocked and opened.

'You are now entering the main hall.'

The pompous announcement made her laugh but her attention was immediately captured by the beautifully patterned tiles on the floor, a brilliant blending of terracotta, green and gold, all brought richly to life by the flood of light from the skylight windows above. The hallway itself was about three metres wide and ran the length of the top level, ending in a staircase which led down to the room with the glass gable. Judy could actually see the tennis-court from the front doorway and the sense of spaciousness was absolutely stunning.

'Marvellous,' she murmured, 'but how are they going to heat all this open area?'

'Hot water-pipes under the slab,' came the matter-of-fact answer. He moved forward to open a door on their right. 'Here we have the master suite, its windows, you will note, facing the east to catch the morning sun.'

It was unfurnished but the floors of the bedroom and dressing-room had been carpeted in a frosted apricot which was a softer shade of the terra-cotta in the tiles. The *en suite* bathroom was sheer luxury, all marble and mirrors and gold fittings. The large spa-bath provoked a sigh of envy.

'That would be heaven after a day's work,' she commented dreamily.

'Mmm. I rather fancy it myself. Nothing like a tub for two. Shall we climb in to see if we fit comfortably?'

Her look said he was an incorrigible optimist. 'On with the tour,' she insisted.

To the left of the hallway were two guest-suites carpeted in the same apricot but again unfurnished. They were good-sized rooms without having the extravagance of space which character-ised the master-suite.

'No critical comment?' One eyebrow was raised in expectation.

Judy had noted the absence of shelving. 'I take it the owner doesn't have children.'

'No. But wouldn't these rooms do if the house was sold to a family?'

'With a bit of adjustment,' she agreed.

'Right. Now to the lower level.'

When they reached the head of the stairs Judy paused, wanting to take in everything from this viewing angle. The carpet below her was a lustrous olive green and on the side-wall to her right rose a huge sandstone chimney, housing a massive fireplace. Again there was no furniture.

'Dining room to the left of the staircase with easy access to the kitchen. Living room on the right,' came the ready explanation.

In her mind's eye Judy could see how it would all look, beautiful leather chesterfields around the fire, a dining room setting of richly polished wood, and always the magnificent view of the outside.

'You don't like?'

'Oh, I like it all right. Very, very much,' she breathed with feeling.

He proceeded to show her the kitchen and laundry, both of which were masterfully designed to provide economy of movement within plenty of work-space. Judy could find nothing to criticise despite every encouragement to do so by her eager guide.

'Well, maybe you'll find something wrong with the other wing,' he twinkled at her. 'I shall be most disappointed if you don't find some fault with Malcolm Stewart's brain-child.'

They crossed the main living area and Judy saw that there were doors on either side of the stone fireplace. The one closest to the glass gable was casually dismissed.

'The owner's study. Can't take you in there. Private sanctum. But I can show you this side.'

Judy was ushered into another bedroom. This one was furnished and very obviously lived in since the bed was unmade.

'My quarters for the present.' He opened another door. '*En suite* bathroom which doubles as a downstairs powder room.'

'And where does the other door lead?' Judy asked, pointing across the room.

'Owner's study again.'

'All very convenient,' Judy nodded, comprehending the easy liveability in the design.

He strolled over to the south-facing window and beckoned to her. 'Look! There's the tree we planted.'

She joined him without even the niggling suspicion of an ulterior motive in his invitation. Her mind was filled with admiration for the architect who had visualised this magnificent house. The position of the tree gave her a pleasant sense of satisfaction. 'It will look pretty there when it grows,' she murmured. 'Make a nice view from the bed.'

'There are views and views, and I like the one I have now. Did you know you had a dimple at the base of your spine?'

His touch sent a ripple of alarm to every nerve-end but her tongue stuck to the roof of her mouth and her breath caught somewhere in her throat as his hands slid around her hips, over her stomach and slowly upwards to cup her breasts. Hard thighs pressed against her and warm lips nuzzled her shoulder.

My God! she thought wildly. This was his parlour and she had walked right into it like a mesmerised little fly. Even now he was weaving a web of sensuality, fingers sliding exploratively under the flimsy material of her bra, finding her nipples and caressing them to hardness. She had to move. Say something. Do something.

But she could feel him moving, growing hard against her softness, and one hand had glided down her body, roaming over her stomach, pressing her back to a vibrant awareness of his arousal. The elastic support of her bikini pants gave way to invasion and then he was touching her, touching her with knowing intimacy, arousing nerve-ends with tantalising skill. And she hadn't done, wasn't doing anything to stop him. Stop him now, a tiny voice of sanity screamed. It was wrong to stand here passively letting him explore her body.

But his touch was gentle, insidiously persuasive, hypnotic, and there was a melting weakness inside her which begged for the caresses to continue. Judy's gaze fixed distractedly on the newly planted tree in the courtyard. It had started out there, the excitement which had promised this physical drowning in pleasure. She had known he could make this happen. She had recklessly flirted with its inevitability. And now . . . now she didn't want to stop anything.

Like a sapling bending with the prevailing wind, her throat swayed to the seductive pressure of his lips. She shivered as his tongue circled her ear-lobe. The hand on her breast slowly withdrew, trailed upwards, fingered its way under her hair. A tug at the halter strings and the tie was undone. A feathery touch down her spine and the support clip gave way. The bra was plucked from her tingling flesh and he was turning her around, pressing her naked torso to his.

She saw the question in his eyes. There was no force intended. But the silken strands of his touch had bound her to this moment and it was too late to break free. The answer was written in the drugged languor of her eyes and the quiver of lips already parted in anticipation.

The question flicked out, burnt into non-existence by a desire so intense that Judy's heart stopped in mid-beat, then galloped wildly as his mouth took hers in avid possession, savouring her surrender with a passion which spun Judy into a feverish response. She wanted him. Wanted this divine madness to go on forever, lifting her out of the ordinariness of day-to-day life.

And suddenly he was lifting her, physically lifting her, fitting her body to his with a sexual emphasis which was unbelievably erotic, the damp thinness of their costumes preventing intimate contact but stimulating almost unbearable excitement. A couple of strides took them to the bed and his weight pinned her underneath him, crushing the breath out of her until he rolled, taking her with him so that they were side by side. And again they kissed, deeply, urgently, while their hands exulted in the freedom to search out and own the strength and the softness.

'Malcolm . . .'

The lilting call was an alien sound, unwelcome, divisive in its impact.

'Oh, hell!' A breath of savage frustration.

'Malcolm . . . are you there?'

High heels clicking on the tiled hallway. Tense silence broken by an angry whisper.

'I left the bloody key in the front door. Stay here. I'll get rid of her.'

Judy lay frozen to the spot, stunned by the sharp interruption and too confused by the circumstances to say or do anything. The man who had so nearly become her lover levered himself off the bed and threw her a searing look of command before crossing to the door.

'I'll be right with you, Viv. I was just about to take a shower,' he lied with casual ease.

It only took a moment for him to step into the *en suite* bathroom and wrap a towel around his waist. Then he was gone from the bedroom, the door clicking firmly shut behind him.

CHAPTER THREE

JUDY shivered. The heat of desire had been abruptly chilled and her body seemed to be jangling with twitchy nerve-ends. A cold wave of sanity slapped her mind, forcing an appraisal of the situation. Surrendering to the temptation of the moment had been crazy enough, but to lie here, cold-bloodedly waiting for a sexual encounter was a complete abandonment of her moral principles. This was sex, a purely physical connection and not by any stretch of the imagination could it come under the heading of love.

The awful part was she still wanted him. His touch was magic and never before had she felt such a strong response to a man. You only live once, she argued, trying to head off the worms of conscience, but the worms wriggled around her mind, insisting that such behaviour was inexcusable. To wilfully go to bed with a man who was a virtual stranger ... to stay in his bed waiting for him ... no, she could not do it. She was acting like a promiscuous little tart and that was precisely what he would think of her. An easy lay. A nice bit of tail for the afternoon.

Goading herself with such thoughts Judy gritted her teeth and moved her sluggish limbs. She could not remain here. Not even in this room. He would start making love to her again and she could not trust herself with him. A hot rush of shame burnt her cheeks as she hitched up her bikini pants. To allow so much intimacy had been bad enough without inviting more. Her legs were shaky with reaction but she walked determinedly over to the window and retrieved her bra from the floor. The flimsy garment did not afford much protection but wearing it was a statement of denial. She was not, and never had been, easy meat for sexual fun and games.

It would be too embarrassing to go out into the living room if the visitor was still there. Judy crossed to the door which led into the owner's study, remembering the glass doors which gave access to the terrace. She half-expected it to be locked since the study was a private domain but the handle turned easily in her hand. She stepped quickly into the room, intending only to use it as a passageway to the terrace, but her eye was suddenly caught and held by the large diorama on the desk.

The three-dimensional model had been built in amazing detail and it was startlingly familiar. Curiosity drove Judy to examine it more closely. The neatly printed names jumped up at her. 'Fairway Beach Tourist Centre. Architect— Malcolm Stewart.' A memory clicked into place. The photograph in the local newspaper had been of this model. But what was it doing here in this house? In the owner's study? Unless Malcolm Stewart, the architect, was also the owner.

Malcolm. That was the name the woman had called out. Malcolm Stewart. The visitor had expected the architect to be here but there was only the man. The man who had been with Judy all day. And he had answered the call in a tone of familiarity, Viv, not Mrs or Miss. Would a labourer, a casual handyman, address a friend of

Malcolm Stewart by her personal name? The man had evaded giving Judy his name. Twice. She had not attached any significance to the evasion but now . . . a sickening apprehension knotted her stomach.

Oh God! It fell together. The whole damned sequence of events; his amusement at her comments on architects, the teasing over her opinions of the house, the fact that he obviously had free run of the place, even to planting the tree wherever he liked. And over and above everything else was the blatant pace of the flirtation which had led to the bed in the adjoining room.

A man of Malcolm Stewart's social standing would not be interested in pursuing a relationship with a little nobody, a turf-deliverer. He had fancied her and she had shown herself vulnerable to his attractions. A brief and pleasurable dalliance to round off the day's work . . . that's all she would have represented to him. Hello and goodbye. Thanks for the memory. It was fun. Even funnier because she had believed he was a nobody too.

Judy cringed at the thought of all the secret laughter he had enjoyed at her expense. Pride slowly began to assert itself, pushing the hurt aside and demanding that she balance the scales. The immense ego of Malcolm Stewart should at least be bruised, and somehow it had to be done lightly, with finesse, so he would not be sure if she was really getting at him. To leave him wondering and well and truly frustrated would go a long way to evening the score.

'Don't you know what happens to little girls who go wandering into forbidden rooms?'

The tone was light but when Judy glanced around the green eyes were sharply observant. She smiled and proceeded to allay any suspicion that she had guessed his identity. 'Is your beard blue?'

'Pardon?' He was puzzled.

She laughed. 'I thought you were referring to Bluebeard who murdered his curious wives.'

He visibly relaxed, strolling towards her with a confident grin on his face. The towel had been discarded but the brief swimming-costume was still in place. Judy tensed as he slid an arm around her shoulders but forced herself into pliancy when he tucked her against his body. Warm lips grazed over her hair.

'Was I so long?' came the soft murmur.

'Long enough for me to get restless,' she answered carelessly and waved a hand over the model. 'This is Malcolm Stewart's work, too. Why didn't you tell me he owned the house?'

'You didn't ask. And it wasn't relevant. Only this is relevant.'

He turned her into an embrace. Judy lifted her arms and curled them around his neck. Her long lashes fluttered a coy invitation. His hands curved under her bottom in familiar possession. Judy's smile was deliberately provocative.

'You're an extremely sexy man, but I'm sure you don't need to be told that,' she purred.

'It's always nice to be told.' He grinned and his grin was full of smug satisfaction.

'You even made me forget my golden rule.'

One eyebrow rose in lazy mockery. 'Rules are so boring.'

'Oh, I agree. So much more exciting to be carried away. But life has a habit of playing dirty tricks, especially with pleasure. That's why I make it a rule never to go to bed with a man unless he can show me a medical clearance.'

'A what?' he asked incredulously.

Judy pouted. 'Well, surely you understand what with herpes and other inconvenient diseases running rampant, casual sex like this just isn't on, is it? I mean, I don't know who you've been bedding lately and a man as hot as you doesn't go without, so really, it would be stupid of me to take the risk, wouldn't it? Unless of course you have a medical certificate stating that . . .'

'My God!' His lips curled with distaste and he abruptly let her go.

'There's no reason to feel like that,' Judy said plaintively. 'Surely you can see the sense of taking care of your health. It's not that I don't fancy you . . .'

He pulled her arms down and almost pushed her away. 'I wouldn't dream of letting you run the risk of contamination,' he bit out sarcastically.

'Oh good! I'm glad you understand,' Judy declared, apparently oblivious to his sarcasm. 'I didn't want to offend you because I've truly enjoyed your company today. Let's go out and have another swim.'

He muttered something vicious under his breath and strode over to open the glass doors on to the terrace. Judy pranced past him with every appearance of looking forward to enjoying herself. There was a guttural clearing of throat behind her.

'Look! Let's give the swim a miss if you don't mind. The visitor who called had some instructions for me and I'd better get on with carrying them out.'

Her secret laughter fizzled into a very damp squib. Anger began a swift burn. The bastard! The self-serving bastard! He didn't even have the grace to pretend that she had any value apart from sexual gratification. The charm, the witty humour, the flirtatious caress of eyes and words; all switched off, a waste of time and energy. She had rung the bell on him and playtime was over. Finis. Exit Judy. Well, she seethed, he could have an exit to remember.

She swung slowly around to face him, mustering all the dignity that her small stature could achieve. Her eyes were a blue blaze of contempt. 'Yes, of course you must get on with your work,' she clipped out with icy disdain. 'I quite understand that your sport is over for the day. You won't mind if I don't apologise for spoiling it for you . . . Mr Stewart.'

She turned on her heel and marched along the terrace, a small figure of trembling rage. She snatched up her towel from the edge of the pool and slammed the door of the change-room behind her. Having thrust her arms into shirt-sleeves and dragged on her shorts, Judy was out again, the bang of the door testifying that her rage had not abated one whit.

He was still standing outside the glass doors of the study, arms akimbo, an amused smile curving his lips as Judy approached. He was deliberately blocking her path to the truck and self-respect demanded that she make no attempt at forcing her way past him. She came to a halt, her chin lifted in proud challenge.

'Don't you have work to do, Mr Stewart?' she

snapped, even further incensed by his amusement.

He sighed and waved a hand in a gesture of dismissal. 'All right. You got me. That was a fair old punch in the gut and I reckon it makes us about even.'

'Nothing makes us even, Mr Stewart, but if I made you feel lousy I'm glad, because I don't happen to be a little whore that you can use for the afternoon and throw aside.'

The amusement was wiped from his face. 'I didn't imagine you were. At least, not until you suggested the kind of promiscuity I find repulsive. I'm sorry that I was fooled into thinking that, even for a moment. I'm also sorry that you feel so hurt by a deception I thought harmless.' He paused, lifting his hands in a gesture of appeal. 'I am the same man, no matter what my name, and it was extraordinarily pleasant to be accepted as a person instead of a personage.'

His apology softened her temper but nothing could assuage her hurt. She had liked him, really liked him, and he was way beyond her reach in any social sense. 'Yes. Well, I daresay you found the situation very titillating. Now if you'll just step aside, I'll be on my way.'

'I don't want you to go. Not like this,' he insisted quitely.

'Why not?' His pose of caring sparked a fiery resentment. 'Why pretend? The clock had to strike midnight sooner or later. Compared to you I'm a pumpkin and I don't have a fairy godmother to wave a magic wand and turn me into a society princess. So why don't you hop back into your castle? Someone else might call and find you slumming it with the turf-deliverer.'

'For God's sake . . .!'

'No! For my sake!' she retorted fiercely. 'You've had your fun. At least have the decency to admit it's over and get out of my way.'

He took stock of her belligerent determination then folded his arms and struck an equally belligerent pose, chin lifted in lofty challenge. 'So! You're an inverted snob. Won't have anything to do with a man who's made a successful career for himself. Too good for the likes of you, am I?'

It was precisely what she had expected him to think. What her experience with David Barker had taught her to expect. For Malcolm Stewart to state it so bluntly had jolted Judy for a moment, but she quickly recovered. He was famous as well as rich, and despite Judy's strong sense of self-worth, she was not so naïve as to think Malcolm Stewart would see her as anything but a little bit of fluff on the side. When it came to serious relationships or social mixing, people like him stuck to his own kind.

'I'm not the snob,' she flung at him with pointed emphasis. 'And I didn't say you were too good for me.'

One eyebrow rose. 'Didn't you? Funny how I got that impression. It so happens that I'm not a snob either. I take people as I find them. And now, since we've got that established, I can't see that you'd have any objection to accompanying me to a dinner-party tonight.'

The wind was completely cut from her sails. Judy stared at him in disbelief. A dinner-party? A public acknowledgement that he was interested in little Judy Campbell? Then scepticism rose in a bitter wave. 'You're only saying that for effect.

No one turns up at a planned dinner-party with an uninvited guest. It isn't done in the best of social circles, is it?'

He sighed. 'Judy, will you get down off that high-horse for a moment?'

Her expression remained obdurate.

He shook his head in exasperation. 'No, it isn't done. But while you were trespassing in my study, thinking evil thoughts about me, I was chatting up my hostess for tonight. She very graciously declared that it was no trouble at all to set another place at her table. Of course I was assuming that you'd want to be with me, but at the time of Viv's untimely interruption, it did seem a reasonable assumption. Was I so wrong?' he added softly.

Judy could not stop the rush of blood which scorched across her cheeks. The memory of their intimacy was all too sharp. And if what he said was true, she had misjudged him and his motives. Shame and embarrassment made her feel very small indeed. She raked an agitated hand through her tumbled hair. It was difficult to adjust to this new perspective of him.

'You really want to ... to ... I mean ... you weren't just ... having a game with me?' she dragged out painfully.

He sighed and stepped forward, drawing her stiffly resistant body into a loose embrace. One hand stroked her cheek with affectionate tenderness and the look in his eyes denied any deception whatsoever. 'I've enjoyed your company. I like you. I want you to be with me tonight. Will you come?'

Judy's heart flipped over. She wanted desperately to say yes, but she knew how vulnerable she was to this man and there were too many questions bombarding her mind. 'You really want me to partner you among your friends?'

'They're only people,' he said drily.

'Yes, but ...' She floundered, finding it too difficult and embarrassing to explain her uncertainties. She had always led a simple, unsophisticated life. Malcolm Stewart's friends were not likely to view her as an acceptable addition to their dinner-party. Her dress would be wrong. Their conversation would exclude her. She would be shown up as a gauche little oddity in their polished society. And he would see that she didn't fit. The green eyes would lose their twinkle and grow critical. 'No. No, thank you,' she said in a despairing rush. 'It's very kind of you to ask me. I appreciate the ...'

'Hey there,' he interrupted and gently lifted her chin so that she was forced to meet his disturbingly direct gaze. 'What's the problem?'

'I haven't anything suitable to wear.' The excuse gabbled off her tongue and even Judy recognised how limp it sounded.

'If that's all that's worrying you, let's get moving. There's still time to catch the shops.'

He was pulling her into the study before she could gather wits enough to make a protest. 'It's Saturday afternoon. They're all shut.'

He grabbed his wallet and a set of keys out of a drawer. 'Not at the beaches. It's the tourist season, remember. Come on. We'll go in my car.'

He bustled her out of the study and through the house, forcing her to take the stairs two at a time to keep up with his pace.

'This is crazy!' she cried as he thrust her out on to the front porch and locked the doors.

'Rubbish! It'll be fun,' he grinned and raced her over to the garages where he pushed her into the passenger seat of an Aston Martin.

He was behind the wheel and accelerating out of the courtyard while Judy was still in a state of befuddled shock. Only slowly did she grasp her bearings. Here she was in an expensive sports car driven by Malcolm Stewart who was intent on . . . God only knew what his intentions were, but she could not allow him to buy her a dress. That would put their relationship on a very dubious footing. On the other hand, her cupboard was distinctly bare of fashionable clothes and if she was going out to dinner with Malcolm Stewart . . . Her eyes raked his profile, still amazed that he had actually made the invitation.

He threw her a triumphant grin. 'I know exactly the place for a smart little number. I scouted the shops at all the beaches on the Central Coast before designing the tourist centre for Fairway.'

'I'll pay you back the money tonight,' she blurted out self-consciously.

'You do that,' he drawled. 'I'd hate you to feel beholden to me. I can plainly see that equality must be upheld at all costs, or that fertile mind of yours will start seeding unworthy thoughts.'

A smile tugged at the corners of her mouth. 'Well, you've already enjoyed one unfair advantage today. I don't aim to let you have any more.'

He slanted his eyebrows in comical appeal. 'Am I forgiven?'

Her smile was coaxed into fullness. 'I guess so.'

'That doesn't sound very definite.'

'I'm still getting used to the idea.'

'I did mean to lead into the subject with more

... ummh ... circumspection and ... uh ... delicacy.'

'Like how?'

'Oh ... like now that we know each other so well, you can call me Mal.'

'Mal?' she repeated mockingly.

He wrinkled his nose at her. 'Rotten name, isn't it? I liked Punch much better. Don't know why you didn't take to it. Brilliant improvisation.'

His words recalled the zany tomfoolery he had indulged in all day and suddenly the situation seemed so absurd that laughter bubbled up her throat and spilled out in hysterical little bursts. 'Are you always this mad?' she finally gasped.

'No,' he grinned. 'The madness only started this morning when Daisy Mae turned up delivering turf. I've felt positively schizophrenic all day. Being me and not me, you understand. It was so delightfully diverting I couldn't resist the temptation to carry it on as long as I could.' He reached for her hand and gave it a friendly squeeze. 'I really didn't mean to upset you, Judy, and you have to admit that you wouldn't have been nearly so open with me if you'd known my name.'

She sighed. 'I just hope your ears burned a couple of times.'

'Nope. But they sure tingled in anticipation.'

It provoked another smile from her. He was the same. He had not changed from the man he had been all day. Her fears and doubts were lulled into abeyance. Malcolm Stewart—Mal— really did like her. He wanted to be with her. A warm glow of happiness settled around Judy's heart.

It was almost five o'clock by the time they reached the shopping centre at Tergola Beach. Fortunately there was a parking space at the kerb right outside the door of 'Panache'. Mal bounded around the car to help Judy out and hurry her into the boutique. The salesgirl eyed him with measuring interest as they entered and showed herself eager to be of help, despite the lateness of their arrival.

'We need a dinner-dress to knock everybody's eyes out,' Mal declared.

'I'm a ten,' Judy added helpfully.

'I'll vouch for that. Ten out of ten,' came the knowing whisper in her ear.

'Size ten, you idiot,' she hissed back at him, a tell-tale blush blooming on her cheeks.

The salesgirl drew out three dresses from an overcrowded rack and hung them on a railing outside the fitting-room. 'These are the best we have to offer . . . in the knockout category,' she added, fluttering her eyelashes coquettishly.

Mal did not seem to notice. He was giving the dresses his full consideration. 'Try on the blue one,' he advised.

It was crocheted silk and Judy suspected that it was hideously expensive. 'How much is it?' she asked, not wanting to commit herself to a garment she could not afford.

'They're very reasonably priced,' the salesgirl assured her, fumbling around to find the ticket.

'Come on. Into the fitting-room. Can't be holding the lady up when it's closing-time,' Mal urged and virtually shoved Judy into the cubicle. The curtain was zipped shut.

'I need the dress,' Judy cried in protest.

'Ah yes, the dress,' he muttered. 'Just getting it

off the hanger. Coming in now.'

He opened the curtain enough to pass the dress to her, then closed it with a firm snap of the wrist. Judy hastily discarded her shirt, shorts and bikini-bra. The blue silk slid over her head. The dress looked shapeless until she pulled in the tie-waist. The gently bloused bodice suddenly achieved a soft elegance and the skirt's diamond-patterned flare showed its cleverness of line. Judy did a slow pirouette in front of the mirror. It was a lovely dress, the kind of dress which could be worn with confidence to any dinner-party, however formal. The low, round neckline was not too low. Suggestive rather than provocative, Judy decided, running a tentative finger over the bare swell of her breasts.

'Like it?' Mal's voice came through the curtain.

'It's beautiful.'

'Good! I'll pay for it while you change back.'

Judy quickly stripped off and looked for the price-ticket, feeling apprehensive but determined to have the dress at any cost. 'I can't find the ticket,' she called out.

'It fell off out here. Fifty-three dollars. Okay?'

A relieved smile lit her face. 'Yes, that's fine.'

'Pass me the dress. I'll get it packed up.'

The shopgirl was beaming at Mal when Judy emerged from the fitting-room. Either she was inordinately pleased with a last-minute sale or Mal had been indulging in his heady brand of charm. He thanked the girl with a flashing smile, handed Judy a plastic bag and led her out to the Aston Martin without a moment's delay. As Judy slid into the passenger-seat she noticed the salesgirl at the door of the shop, gazing at the car and its owner with naked envy.

Judy waited until Mal was seated. Then with a tilt of the head in the girl's direction, asked sardonically, 'Do you chat up every woman you meet?'

He grinned unashamedly. 'If it gets me what I want.'

The cynical purpose behind those words gave Judy pause for thought. Malcolm Stewart was very charming, very attractive and very aware of his impact on the female sex. The additional charisma of wealth and success made that impact even more potent. And his choice of women limitless. Judy was way out of her league with such a man, and while he undoubtedly found her attractive today, she would be foolish to expect the attraction to be anything but brief.

Swim with the tide. The words echoed through her mind and brought a grim smile to her lips. Earlier this afternoon she had not known that the tide covered such a dangerous undertow. The swift current of passion which had swept her into Malcolm Stewart's bed would have to be diverted tonight . . . somehow. He wanted her. Maybe that was all he wanted and the rest was words, glib words which had flattered her into giving him another chance. 'Be with me tonight,' he had said, and he had probably meant all night.

And tomorrow? What would she feel tomorrow if he waved her goodbye with a, 'Been nice knowing you. Maybe we can do it again sometime.' Never had she been so strongly attracted to a man but if she gave herself to him and he casually discarded her like a used article . . . No. That was only inviting the worst kind of hurt. She was not going to be another easy conquest for him, a pleasant memory easily forgotten. If he really liked her as a person, then let him prove it without a headlong rush into bed.

A strong hand took one of hers from her lap and fondled it with slow deliberation. 'You're very quiet. Not having second thoughts are you, Judy?'

'Lots of them,' she admitted, throwing him a look full of irony. 'You're a bit rich for my blood, Malcolm Stewart, but I guess I'll survive one night out with you.'

'Maybe you'll acquire a taste for me,' he suggested with a teasing flash of wicked green eyes. 'You'd better give me road directions to where you live,' he added more seriously. 'I don't want to waste time getting lost.'

Melinga Creek was a forty-minute drive in the truck from his house. The Aston Martin would slash ten minutes from that time but the round trip would still take an hour. 'Where is the dinner-party being held?' she asked, hoping that the home in question was situated at a more convenient distance.

'Not far from my place. Just over at Kinsela Valley.'

Even further away. He would not find a long drive late at night an attractive proposition, particularly as it would mean curtailing his alcohol intake to the 0.05 legal limit for driving. Ever since the regulation had been introduced, most people on a social outing organised a non-drinking driver or an overnight stay which precluded the risk of police arrest. Judy did not want to be pressured into an overnight stay for any reason.

'It's too far for you to pick me up,' she said decisively. 'I'll drive to your house and you can take me from there. What time should I arrive?'

His frown expressed disapproval but he did not argue. 'Ten to eight should be soon enough.'

They drove the rest of the way in silence. It was not until Mal was escorting Judy down to her truck that he spoke again.

'Are you making a statement of independence, Judy, or don't you trust me to get you home safely?'

She glanced at him in surprise, not having expected him to chew over her decision.

'You do intend to come?' he added with dry insistence.

'I didn't buy a dress for nothing,' she answered lightly. 'And as for the driving, I like to keep my options open. Call it independence if you like.'

His smile had a wry twist. 'I don't like. It's less time I have with you. But I suspect you've made up your mind about it so I'll just claim a reminder to see me through until you return.'

'A reminder?'

They had reached the truck but before Judy could open the door she was whirled around. With her balance upset she literally fell against the hard chest and the arms which encircled her had no intention of letting her go.

'We were very rudely interrupted,' he murmured, and his kiss melted every sensible resolution Judy had made.

She clung like a limpet to him even when he eased back from the passionate intensity which had seduced her again. It was positively humiliating to find that her legs felt like jelly and her heart was trumpeting its disordered pulse. A shudder ran through her as he smiled the smug smile which told her all too clearly that she had given satisfaction. She was putty in his hands, spineless putty, and if she did not put some stiffening in her spine soon, there was no way of countering the effect he had on her.

'Ten to eight. If you're a minute late I'll come hunting for you,' he warned.

Hunting. Like a predator. And she was his prey. No, dammit! She was no one's prey. 'I'm always punctual,' she tossed at him and climbed into the truck.

It was quite miraculous that she did not crash the gears or do anything spectacularly awful as she reversed up the track. Pure instinct carried her off with every semblance of a driver in complete control of her vehicle. Control of her body was a long time in coming and Judy wondered if she had the will-power to resist a force which could hit her with such unreasoning power. Somehow she had to erect some necessary defences between now and tonight.

CHAPTER FOUR

JUDY felt absurdly self-conscious as she walked down the hallway to the living-room where her family was watching television. Although she had announced that she was going to a party and would not want dinner, her parents would have assumed that it was the usual jeans and T-shirt party common to her age-group. Since arriving home she had shut herself in bathroom and bedroom, determined to create the image of a glossy, social butterfly. She had no doubt that many a beautiful woman had graced Malcolm Stewart's arm, and while Judy was not cast in the cover girl mould, she had enough natural assets to present herself with considerable style.

She had washed and blow-dried her hair to the smoothness required for a fashionably loose chignon on top of her head. The tendrils which escaped confinement fell into natural ringlets around her ears and neck and lent the hairstyle a more positive femininity. She had experimented with extra make-up around her eyes but the emphasis had only served to obliterate her other features. Her eyes dominated her small face as it was and she had hastily wiped off the frosted eye-shadow and resigned herself to a pearly-pink mouth and the lightest touch of mascara.

The narrow shoulder-straps of the blue dress, its low neckline and her upswept hair combined to show too large an expanse of bare, golden skin. Judy's only good jewellery was a fine silver locket and matching braclet. She had clipped them on and then worried about being too formally dressed. Fortunately the casual elegance of her one pair of high-heeled sandals played down the formal look. Even so, she knew her parents would be surprised at her appearance and a light flush stole over her cheeks as she pushed open the living room door.

'Why, Judy! How lovely you look! I haven't seen that dress before.' Astonishment and pleasure mingled on Tess Campbell's face, wiping out the tired lines of age.

Judy did her best to shrug off her embarrassment. 'I bought it this afternoon. I'm going now. Is it all right if I take the Commodore, Dad?'

He beamed with pride. 'Dressed like that, my love, you could take the Rolls Royce if I owned one. Who's the man who forced you out of the jeans brigade?' he teased.

Judy's flush grew brighter. 'No one you've met, Dad.'

'Well, tell him he has my gratitude. It's a rare pleasure to see my darling daughter dressed as a real woman.'

'Yeah! You look really beautiful, Sis,' Billy chimed in, his eyes rounded with childlike wonder at the unexpected transformation.

'Thanks for the compliments,' she said quickly, anxious to make a retreat before any more pertinent questions were levelled at her. 'I don't know when I'll get home but don't worry. And thanks for the car, Dad.'

'Have a good time,' her mother called after her.

'I will,' Judy replied lightly and hoped that it would be true.

It was not like her to be secretive yet she felt strangely reluctant to reveal anything about Malcolm Stewart to her family. Within a few hours she had been swamped with too many emotions and it would have been difficult to talk about him without showing some of the turmoil he had aroused in her. She could not have pretended that tonight's outing was merely a casual invitation. It means too much.

Too much, she warned herself cautiously. All she really knew was that Malcolm Stewart was physically attracted to her, but he had more than sex appeal for her. And she did not want it to end in his bed tonight. She did not want it to end at all. If sex was all he wanted from her, then the primrose path would lead on to hell, because once having given herself, it was not in Judy's nature to walk lightly away.

Everything had happened too fast this afternoon. She had been caught up in a sudden whirlwind, but now there was no excuse for walking blindly into the whirlwind again. She knew it was there. The excitement beckoned her, but an abrupt drop from the heights would leave her tattered and broken. Better to hold back and see if Malcolm Stewart was interested enough in her company to pursue a relationship without the gratification of easy-come sex.

The intensity of her thoughts had taken her attention from driving. Suddenly aware that she had been stuck behind a slow-moving car for too long, Judy glanced anxiously at the clock on the dash-board. Seven-forty. Ten minutes to get there. She wondered if he really would hunt her up if she was not punctual and decided it was highly unlikely that Malcolm Stewart could offend his friends for her sake.

It was seven-fifty-five when she turned the Commodore into his driveway. She accelerated up to the gravelled courtyard, hoping that he was ready and waiting for her. Five minutes late was only a small delay but it was only good manners to arrive on time for a dinner-party and she did not want to invite criticism.

Malcolm Stewart emerged from the garage as she parked in the car-port on the other side of the house. The sight of his welcoming smile started a flutter in Judy's heart. She took a deep breath and counselled down-to-earth common sense, whereupon she stepped out of the Commodore and sensibly locked it.

'Sorry I'm late. I was trapped in some slow traffic,' she explained hastily.

Her heart was not responding to orders. Malcolm Stewart had been fascinating in the flesh but in clothes he was positively devastating. It seemed unfair that one man should have so much going for him. He wore no tie but the green silk shirt shrieked of money and the fawn linen trousers were the last word in fashionable tailoring. Class was written all over him from the burnished copper hair to the undoubtedly hand-made leather loafers on his feet. More sharply than ever, Judy felt he was way out of her league.

'I was just about to scour the countryside for you,' he declared, the green eyes sweeping over her with obvious appreciation. 'I'm glad I didn't have to, and you were certainly worth waiting for. You look even more entrancing, if that's possible.'

'Well, I guess I'd even give you ten out of ten tonight,' she retorted flippantly, trying to repress the shiver of awareness which shot through her as he took her elbow and steered her towards the Aston Martin.

'I'm relieved to know that my defects are hidden.'

His grin denied any worry over defects and July decided it was wiser to lead away from a conversation which had physical overtones. She held her tongue while he saw her seated but became completely unnerved when he sat in the driver's seat and made no move to start the car.

'Why are you staring at me? Is something wrong?'

'I'm wondering why the hell we're going out when all I want to do is take you inside and make love to you.'

His directness floored her for a moment. Then two angry spots of colour fired her cheeks and her tongue lashed out in attack. 'Is that all you want?'

His quick frown registered puzzlement and the green eyes measured the hostility in hers. 'What do you want?' he asked softly.

She turned away, unable to hold his questioning gaze without revealing her vulnerability. 'I don't know,' she finally dragged out. 'It's crazy my even being here with you.'

He took her hand and to her intense mortification it trembled as he fondled it. 'You want me just as much as I want you,' he stated quietly.

It was true. She did want him. She was torn with a desire which threatened to overturn every moral principle she had cherished. It took a tremendous effort of will to snatch her hand away from the insidious seduction of his touch. 'We'll be late. You can't just not turn up to a dinner-party,' she gabbled out defensively, then threw him a frightened look of appeal. 'I hardly know you.'

His smile held a twist of irony. 'Is my name such a stumbling-block?'

Judy's cheeks burned even more painfully at the oblique reference to her earlier wantonness and again she turned away.

He sighed. 'You're right. We'd better go. Otherwise Viv will be charging around to find out why I haven't shown up.'

The Aston Martin throbbed into noisy life and Judy had time to digest that last remark before the powerful engine settled into a gentle purr. The woman had come to his house this afternoon, alone and apparently uninvited, and Mal had just suggested that their hostess would be so upset by his absence that she would leave her other guests to round him up.

'Who is this Viv?' she asked bluntly.

'Vivien Holgate. Her husband is my solicitor.'

The answer was matter-of-fact, telling Judy nothing except that the woman was married. 'Does she fancy you?' she asked even more bluntly.

He slanted a quizzical eyebrow at her. 'Now what made you ask that question?'

'Why don't you answer it?'

He sighed and returned his attention to the road. 'She is beginning to make herself a little too obvious, and I don't like being chased.'

No, he wouldn't, Judy privately mused. He was a hunter who liked to make his own terms. 'Do you fancy her?' she asked curiously.

A little smile curled his lips. 'It would be

difficult not to fancy Viv. She's quite a woman.
But married women are a hassle and I happen to
like Bill. He's a damned good solicitor, and
they're not easy to come by.'

Not as easy as married women, Judy finished
sourly. She didn't like the flavour of his answer.
Not one bit. Maybe his invitation to the party
had been prompted by a desire to put another
woman between him and his hostess, thereby
killing two birds with one stone, satisfying his
desire for Judy and putting off the other woman
. . . or allaying her husband's suspicions. If Mal
really fancied Vivien Holgate . . .

'I don't like your silences,' he said abruptly
and took hold her hand, this time in a firmly
possessive grip. 'I can feel you putting distance
between us.'

'There is a distance between us,' she muttered.

'Only in your mind. Not in mine,' he argued.
'And just in case you've started harbouring evil
thoughts again, it's you I want, not Vivien
Holgate. Got that?'

She smiled, relieved by his assurance and
amused by the uncanny perception which had
prompted it.

He threw her a quick grin. 'I can't very well
slap her down if she insists on flirting with me.
I'm stuck with being courteous because I do
business with Bill.'

'How terrible for you!' she teased. 'One of the
perils of being a ten.'

He gave her hand a gentle squeeze. 'That's
better. Don't lose your sense of humour, Judy. I
love it.'

I want you to love all of me. The words slid
into her mind and surprised her. She looked at

him in undisguised wonder and he caught the look.

'Now what?' he asked in a bedevilled tone.

'Nothing . . . nothing,' she repeated, flustered by the sharpness of her feeling. She had only just now concluded that she knew too little about him. It was ridiculous to fancy herself in love with him. He was handsome, that was all. And funny, and generous, and . . . and it was sheer pie in the sky to dream that he might fall in love with her. Apple pie. That's what she was. And he had probably been knocking back strawberry torte for years.

'Tell me what you're thinking,' he demanded, throwing her a stern look.

'Is it only the Holgates?' she asked in quick prevarication.

'No. Two other couples. The Davises, Larry and Felicity. He's in real estate. One of the developers behind the Fairway Tourist Centre. She's a friend of Viv's. And the Hagans. You've probably heard of him. The American novelist, Patrick Hagan?'

She shook her head. 'I don't read many novels.'

'His wife also writes. Ruth Devlin?'

She wrinkled her nose at his expectant look. 'Doesn't ring a bell. As I said, I don't . . .'

'Read many novels. Neither do I, if the truth be told. I designed their house. Never seen a man so besotted with his wife,' he added in an amused tone.

Judy was not amused. 'What's so funny about a man loving his wife?'

'Nothing. It's great. You just don't see it very often. Not so obviously. The funny part is that if you'd read any of his books, you'd never expect it of him. All sex on the run. But there he is, well and truly caught, hook, line and sinker.'

There was no envy in his voice, nothing to suggest he might like a similar fate. Just amusement. He even referred to marriage as being caught. Sex on the run was obviously more to his liking and Judy advised herself to keep that thought firmly in mind.

'He must be very happy with her,' she remarked, unable to resist pointing out that marriage was not such a painful trap. Curiosity prompted her to ask, 'What's she like?'

'Not what you'd call beautiful, but quite attractive. Lovely blue eyes. Though not a match for yours,' he declared with smug bias.

Judy sighed and rolled her eyes at him. 'Can't you get your mind off the physical?'

He grinned. 'Very difficult with you holding my hand.'

'I meant what is she like as a person?'

'Rather reserved. Though not with her husband. I think she might very well be besotted with him. Which I must confess I find oddly touching. It's my experience that few women love their hubands . . .' his eyebrows slanted mockingly, '. . . to the exclusion of all other men.'

Not Vivien Holgate apparently, and there had probably been a lot of married women who had slyly suggested availability to Malcolm Stewart. Not many men could match his obvious attractions and the fact that he was unattached was a challenge in itself.

'My parents love each other,' she said defensively.

'Then you are singularly blessed. Mine certainly didn't.'

The touch of bitterness in his voice stirred her curiosity. 'Divorced?'

'The property wrangle went on for years. The legal fraternity had a ball,' he answered flippantly. 'Though I can't say I suffered from it. Guilt tends to open wallets. I was given the best of everything from both sides, and all the financial support I wanted to set me up as an architect. Makes it easy, doesn't it? To have as much money as you need.'

'I daresay it helps,' Judy agreed quietly. His cynicism about love and marriage was understandable but it sent a shiver of apprehension down her spine. 'All the same, money doesn't generate talent and success only comes with a lot of hard work. I can't imagine it was all so easy for you,' she added thoughtfully.

'You're right. But I love my work. There's nothing more thrilling than watching your own vision grow into reality.'

'I know what you mean.'

The raised eyebrows carried surprise. 'Do you?'

'Well, landscaping gives a similar sense of achievement,' she explained. 'I think it's one of the most pleasure-giving art-forms. A beautifully designed garden in full bloom, a clump of trees and shrubs of varying foliage, even an orchard specifically planted for its show of blossom. It's more ... alive than a building, giving different views all year round.'

'Mmm ... you have a point,' he conceded, giving her a considering look. 'You sound as if you really know what you're talking about, Judy.'

'Well, apart from being in the plant nursery business, I have put in a couple of years' study at a horticultural college,' she said drily.

The eyebrows lifted in surprise. 'Done much landscaping?'

'Some. Not much.' She gave him a wry smile. 'My physique doesn't impress customers.'

He chuckled. 'Oh, I bet it does, Daisy Mae. I bet the wives can't get their men home fast enough.'

She sighed and turned her attention to the property they were now entering. Fences of white railing kept some splendid looking horses in the green paddocks on either side of the driveway to the house. An avenue of silky oaks added distinction but Judy's mouth thinned in grim apprehension as the house came into full view, a huge Tudor house, complete with shuttered windows, turrets and shingled roof. This bit of real estate had to be worth a least half a million dollars and probably a great deal more.

Judy had expected Malcolm Stewart's friends to be wealthy, but the overwhelming evidence of it knotted her stomach with nervous tension. It was bad enough that she would be out of her age-group, and she could probably expect a measure of hostility from the hostess who had anticipated having Malcolm Stewart on his own, but over and above that, was the fear that she would be shown up as being well and truly out of her class.

Australia might be touted as a classless society but there were lines of wealth which effectively separated people in manner and thought. It was not easy to cross those lines without putting a foot wrong and Judy had had no practice at it.

They were not the first to arrive, though not the last either. There was only one car parked in the circular driveway which gave easy access to the front entrance of the house. Judy noted that it was a Volvo, not quite so much of a status symbol as an Aston Martin, but a statement of affluence none the less.

Affluence. Money. She remembered the cheque in her handbag just as Mal braked the car to a halt. 'Here. This is for the dress.' She quickly passed it to him before he opened the door. 'And thanks for the loan.'

He glanced at it, gave her a look of amusement, then folded it and slipped it on to a shelf on the dashboard. 'Account paid. You have a very stubborn streak of independence, Judy Campbell.'

She smiled. 'I like to be my own woman.'

'And if I want to make you mine?'

'I'd have to want it, too,' she answered lightly, pretending that she took his words as flirtation and denying the erratic flutter of her pulse.

'You know, the cavemen had the right idea and you're making me feel increasingly primitive. Let's go back home and forget we were ever invited.'

Sheer cowardice tempted her to agree with him but Judy was determined to at least see more of Malcolm Stewart's life than his bed. 'I'm hungry. You promised me a free dinner and there's one being cooked for us right here.'

He sighed and got out, muttering inaudible words under his breath. Judy laughed at the range of mocking frowns he pulled as he rounded the bonnet to reach her door. The laughter eased her tension and she was in a more relaxed frame of mind when their hostess answered the summons of the door-chimes.

One glance at Vivien Holgate told Judy that anything less stylish than the blue dress would have been a disaster from which she would never have recovered. The woman was the ultimate in current fashion. The cream silk harem pants were topped by a halter garment which seemed to expose more than it covered, and a wide gold belt accentuated the curves of a voluptuous figure. Gold chains and an amber pendant added their allure to a beautiful olive skin. The straight black hair fell thickly to her shoulders, a gold comb sweeping it behind her ear on one side. Her face was not really beautiful but her make-up was a masterpiece of illusion. She looked absolutely stunning and the liquid brown eyes fed hungrily on Malcolm Stewart.

'Hello, darling. Recovered from your labours?'

'Just about hitting my prime,' he answered breezily. 'May I introduce Judy Campbell? Judy, our hostess, Vivien Holgate.'

No hand was offered. In fact both hands were occupied insinuating themselves around Mal's arm. Judy showed her teeth. 'How do you do,' she said in her most cultured voice, wondering if she could outdo Eliza Doolittle.

The brown eyes were not exactly warm with welcome. They browsed over Judy with a semblance of amused interest before lifting to Mal in mocking challenge. 'Did you have to rob the schoolroom?'

'Oh, Judy assures me she's over the age of consent,' he drawled.

'Yes. I've even cast a vote the last few years,' Judy added with an excess of sweetness.

Mal grinned and Vivien showed a flicker of annoyance. Bitch! Judy thought with venom. And she wasn't too pleased with Mal's sexual innuendo either. It was one thing to play word-games in private, quite another to suggest she was his bed-mate in public. The evening had not got off to a good start. She might be outclassed in the financial stakes but she was not going to submit to condescension. Pride insisted that she was as good as anybody and fine feathers did not necessarily clothe fine birds.

'Well, you do look so charmingly young,' came the silky rejoinder from her hostess. 'You'll have to pardon a little envy from one who has to work at it.'

'And may I say you've done a superb job tonight.' Mal slid out the words with all the slickness of a gallantry machine.

The black lashes fluttered down to a level of sultriness. 'Thank you, Malcolm. Do come in. Bill is just mixing the champagne cocktails. We've decided to dine al fresco tonight. It's too hot to be inside and it's such a beautiful evening for a barbecue.'

A barbecue! In those clothes? Judy thought incredulously, but she fixed a smile on her face and was glad that Mal retained hold of her hand as they moved into the foyer. Vivien Holgate was still clinging to his arm and Judy could very well have been relegated to trailing behind them but for his insistent clasp. Vivien was forced to uncling herself at the first doorway.

She led them into a large games-room which featured a full-sized billard table and a much-mirrored bar. Three sets of eyes fixed on Judy, curiosity and assessment gleaming out of all of them. The tall, thin man behind the bar produced a sly little smile. The woman on the bar-stool raised her thinly plucked eyebrows at Vivien. The other man dropped his foot from the brass bar-fender and came forward, a beaming grin all over his fleshy face. He patted the garishly printed Hawaiian shirt which hung loosely over a beer-paunch and white trousers.

'Well, well, well.' He took Judy's free hand in his, pressing it with moist heat. 'Where did you find this lovely, Mal?'

'Down the bottom of my garden,' came the glib answer. 'Judy, this is Larry Davis.'

Larry chortled. 'Bottom of your garden! What fairy-story will you be telling us next? It's a pleasure to make your acquaintance, Judy.'

'Thank you.' It was an effort not to pull away from his sweaty touch and she hoped he would keep his hands to himself for the rest of the evening.

'Back off, Larry,' came his wife's bored instruction. 'Judy who, darling?'

'Judy Campbell,' Mal supplied.

One thin eyebrow arched higher. 'As in the Campbells are coming?'

'Hurrah! Hurrah!' Larry chorused with suggestive enthusiasm.

'Oh, do shut up, Larry. Why would she look at you when she has Malcolm? Just drag your hand out of his, Judy. I'm Felicity, his long-suffering wife.'

'How do you do,' Judy murmured. It seemed to her that Felicity did very well for herself from the look of the rings on the languidly waving hand. The strawberry-blonde curls owed much to the art of a hairdresser and the lime-green sheath was not the product of home-dressmaking. The suffering certainly did not come from a lack of material goods.

The man behind the bar did not wait for an

introduction. 'Hello, Judy. The name is Bill. Good you see you, Mal. Ready for a cocktail?'

'Hope you've used a light hand with the brandy. Those champagne cocktails of yours are hangover specials,' Mal drawled as he steered Judy over to the bar.

Bill grinned. 'Just one to start the evening on a high note. Here you are, Judy.'

She hesitated, eyeing the cocktail warily. 'I think I'll stick to soft drink, if you don't mind, Bill.'

'Soft drink!' Vivien repeated derisively. 'What have you brought us, Malcolm? A temperance lady?'

Judy bridled at the criticism. 'I'm driving,' she explained shortly.

'Don't tell me you're letting a woman behind the wheel of the Aston Martin, Mal,' Larry jibed.

'You'll be all right, Judy. The police never set up the booze-bus on these backroads from here to my place,' Mal assured her.

He was doing it again, only this time he was virtually telling everyone that she was going to spend the night with him, staying at his house, in his bed. 'I prefer to remain sober,' she replied tightly, but right at this moment she could do with a stiff drink. She turned to Bill with a sweet smile. 'I'll have one cocktail, but soft drink after that. Okay?'

'I never argue with a woman. Soft drink it shall be.'

He handed her a glass of sparkling liquid. It was a pink-gold colour. The rim of the glass had been frosted with fine sugar and a cherry floated on top. She sipped the drink experimentally and found it very easy to take. Felicity began droning on about how dreary the alcohol limit was and the door-chimes drew Vivien away. Judy nibbled at the cherry, dipping it into the drink for extra taste. Gradually she became conscious of being watched by her host. She glanced up into cold, grey eyes. They slid from her to Mal and back to her before kindling to a semblance of warmth.

'What should I serve you from now on? Fruit-juice, Coca-Cola, lemon squash?' he asked in a low, flat tone.

'Coca-Cola, thank you,' Judy murmured, anxious not to draw attention from the conversation of the other three.

Bill nodded and gave a thin smile. Judy wondered if he was aware of his wife's infatuation for Malcolm Stewart. That cold, considering look seemed to have been measuring Judy's attraction for the man whom Bill Holgate might view as a rival for his wife's affections. He had shown himself affable enough towards Mal but Judy suspected that the solicitor was a man who held his own counsel and did not readily display emotion.

He wore a conservative cream shirt with equally conservative tan trousers; all in all a conservative man with a wife who was spectacularly flamboyant. A man who would be loath to lose what he had, Judy decided, yet not a man who would countenance adultery.

Was that why Mal had indicated that Judy was his sleeping partner? A wish fulfilment or a deliberate diversion to hide another affair altogether? The blatant charms of Vivien Holgate had undermined Judy's confidence in the sincerity of Mal's declarations. She was not at all sure that he was the type of man who would knock back a temptation which was persistently offered.

Suddenly she felt very alone, very small, and very insignificant. She looked up at Mal who was recounting a funny story to the Davises. There he was, strikingly handsome, brimming over with personality and sex appeal, wealthy, successful ... the lot. However could she have imagined that such a man could really be interested in little Judy Campbell from Melinga Creek?

And he hadn't really been interested, she realised with sharp clarity. He had not asked her any questions about her life. She had given him information but he had not asked for it. His conversation had always revolved around the physical here and now ... and the physical future. And when it came to the physical, Vivien Holgate left Judy Campbell for dead. Vivien Holgate was the type of woman who captured such men. Even as Judy watched Mal his head turned instinctively towards their hostess as she re-entered the room with the last arrivals.

The Hagans made a handsome couple, the man quite striking in an oddly rakish way, the woman very chic in a violet and green dress which was banded around the neck and waist with white. They carried with them an air of contentment which was rather comforting in this company. They looked at Judy with interest, as if pleased to meet someone new, and they greeted her with ready warmth when introduced. Judy felt a twinge of envy at the way Patrick Hagan looked at his wife, a soft caress of love in his expressive brown eyes.

Judy glanced hopefully at Mal, wanting just the vaguest reflection of that look. He was smiling at Vivien Holgate who wore a self-satisfied smirk. A heavy lump settled in Judy's heart.

'Did you have to rob the schoolroom?' The mocking echo ran in her ears and a wash of disillusion swept in the end of the sentence ... 'to find a girl dumb enough not to guess she was being used.'

CHAPTER FIVE

JUDY felt worn out. She had given the performance of her life, a bright sparkling display of
'having a good time'. No one could have possibly
guessed that the effervescent façade hid a hollow
desolation. She had even managed to respond to
Mal's public caresses with every appearance of
pleasure. A couple of times she had caught Ruth
Hagan observing her curiously but a bright smile
had resolved the moments of unease.

She had done very well, but dear God! she was
sick of the whole scene. It was late enough to
suggest going home but Bill Holgate had insisted
the men join him in a game of snooker, so she sat,
sipping her second cup of coffee, vaguely
listening to Vivien and Felicity rehashing a class
reunion which they had recently attended at their
old school.

At least the withdrawal of the men had taken
most of the strain out of the situation. She did
not have to watch Vivien's sly flirtation with Mal,
nor suffer Larry Davis's oafish ogling. If the real
estate man had made one more playful remark
about fairies at the bottom of gardens, Judy
might well have bared her teeth in a manner
which resembled a sabre-toothed tiger.

Her eyes rested sourly on Vivien Holgate. The
bleak truth was that Judy could not even begin to
compete with a woman of Vivien's experience.
Apart from the sense of presence she imparted so
effortlessly, Vivien Holgate was a brilliant hostess.

The barbecue had been like no other barbecue Judy had ever attended. In effect it had been a formal dinner party, transferred from dining room to patio without losing any style whatsoever. They had sat on cushioned chairs of ornate aluminium lace at a glass-topped table which had been set with the finest crystal and silverware. The dinner had been superb; fresh seafoods served with an avocado mousse, a variety of exotic salads to complement the barbecued fillet steak and Idaho potatoes, continental cheesecake and strawberries. Everything had been served with a graceful smoothness which denied any trouble at all, an accomplishment which only came with skill and many years' practice. Even the conversation had been subtly directed so that interest never lagged. Vivien had been simply marvellous at looking after everyone's comfort. Especially Mal's.

Sunk in her brooding reverie, Judy did not hear the question directed at her. She was suddenly, pricklingly aware of being the focus of attention for the other three women. 'I'm sorry. What did you say?'

Vivien Holgate's smile oozed condescension. She was not so concerned now with impressing everyone. The men's attention was directed elsewhere. 'I asked what school did you go to?'

Judy had heard enough of the conversation to be aware that Vivien and Felicity had attended one of the most exclusive private schools in Sydney. For a moment she was tempted to lie, to match their snobbery with the name of a similar institution, but almost instantly the temptation was swept away by a wave of aggression. She did not care what these people thought any more.

Besides, such status symbols had no value to her and she wasn't going to pretend otherwise.

'I went to the local state school,' she stated bluntly.

Felicity raised her eyebrows in disdain. 'How dreary for you!'

Judy's hackles rose higher. 'I didn't find it so. Nor did I consider myself the least bit under-privileged. I enjoyed my school years and I've met a lot of people who hated going to boarding school.'

'Yes. I did,' Ruth Hagan put in quietly. 'In fact I found it very dreary,' she added with a little smile at Judy, a smile which invited the sharing of a private joke.

Judy's lips twitched despite her overall feeling of hostility.

'Oh, but you went to some convent out in the country,' Felicity protested. 'It couldn't provide the advantages of a city school.'

Ruth shrugged. 'I taught in a state school. I much preferred its normal society to the exclusive atmosphere generated in private schools. However, I daresay each has its advantages.' Again she smiled at Judy. 'I've been admiring your lovely dress all night. May I ask where you bought it?'

Ruth Hagan was a nice person. A really nice person. Not like the other women at all. Judy smiled with genuine pleasure. 'It was in a boutique out at Tergola.'

'Oh yes! "Panache",' Felicity drawled. 'I remember seeing those Patelli dresses out there. I thought them too expensive for what they were but that one does look well on you.'

Judy frowned. It seemed absurd that Felicity

Davis should consider fifty-three dollars expensive for any dress. 'You must be mistaken, Felicity. I thought the price very reasonable.'

The trill of laughter was faintly derisive. 'Either you have indulgent parents, my dear, or you have a very lucrative job. I keep telling Larry he's a cheapskate over clothes. He doesn't mind investing in jewellery but he gets quite stroppy when I pay over two hundred and fifty dollars for a dress.'

Over two hundred and fifty! For a moment Judy's mind boggled and then it cleared to bright, crystal sharpness. The hustle into the fitting-room, the ticket which she had never seen, the look on the salesgirl's face . . . oh yes! A fine little charade aimed at solving a problem without fuss. So that Malcolm Stewart could have his own way. Just a simple little lie which Judy had swallowed far too quickly. Had wanted to swallow because the dress had been so perfect. She should have known better.

'Do you work?' Vivien asked her with an air of total disinterest.

'Yes, I work,' Judy bit out. The resentment seething through her was testing her control.

'Well, what do you do for a living?' Vivien pressed on, obviously not caring two hoots what Judy did.

The resentment peaked. To hell with trying to fit into this society! She didn't give a damn any more. 'I deliver turf,' she declared defiantly, and positively enjoyed the shock on their faces.

Ruth was the first to recover. 'You . . . deliver . . . turf?' she repeated incredulously.

'That's right. Rolls and rolls of grass and dirt. Instant lawn for customers. I unload it too,' she added for good measure.

Ruth's grin was one of joyous delight. 'Oh, that's marvellous! Absolutely marvellous!'

'She's pulling our legs, Ruth,' Vivien claimed sarcastically.

Judy rose to her feet, no longer prepared to suffer their brand of chit-chat. 'Ask Mal if you don't believe me. I delivered his back lawn today,' she tossed off as she turned her back on them and strolled into the games room.

As soon as the men finished their snooker match she would demand that Mal take her home. Her gaze darted around the billiard table evaluating the state of the game. With only one red and the colours left, it should not take long to finish. Larry Davis gently tapped the cue-ball. It clipped the red and both balls rolled to a halt on either side of the blue, leaving the next player neatly snookered.

Bill Holgate applauded. 'Well done, Larry. I think that does it, gentlemen. Patrick, you'd need to clear that red and all the colours to win from this point. Do you concede?'

'No fear!' Mal insisted. 'Not without having a go. Patrick, if you angle the cue-ball off the side-cushion and glance the red at the correct angle, you might get it into a top pocket.'

Patrick grinned and shook his head. 'Who do you think I am? Eddie Charlton? No, I think I've had enough snooker for tonight.' Ruth had followed Judy inside. Patrick slid his arm around his wife's shoulders and hugged her to him.

'Come on, Patrick,' Mal urged in a tone of barely repressed annoyance. 'You can manage one more shot.'

'Go on,' Ruth murmured. 'I only came to watch.'

'Haven't got a hope,' Patrick declared and his eyes alighted on Judy with indulgent warmth. 'Here, Judy. You play it for me. You can appease Mal's competitive spirit.'

He passed her the cue. Mal rolled his eyes. Bill and Larry wore triumphant grins.

Judy had been going to refuse, only too relieved that the game was over, but all the condescension she had swallowed tonight suddenly threw up a spurt of defiance. 'All right. Thank you, Patrick. I will have a shot.'

Ever since Billy's illness, Drew Campbell had turned to his daughter as the one child to whom he could pass on his skills. She had become the son he would never have. Her natural ability at the snooker table had pleased her father and he had taught her everything he knew. This was one field of expertise where she was not outclassed by the present company and while she might not be able to make the shot required to keep them in the game, she would show them that she was no amateur to be despised.

She felt the cue for balance while she studied the position on the table. 'Could I have a smaller cue, Bill?' she asked sweetly.

He passed her one and she carefully tested it for balance before giving a nod of compliance. She chalked the tip ready for play.

'Well, Mal, the little lady seems to have some knowledge of the game,' Larry commented jokingly.

'So it would seem. I wouldn't laugh too soon, Larry. Judy is full of surprises,' Mal retorted without any real confidence.

'Do you have a stool I can stand on, Bill?' Judy

asked, playing up the role of little lady with secret relish.

A stool was produced. Vivien and Felicity wandered in to watch. The smirks on their faces suggested a ready anticipation that Judy would make a fool of herself. Judy positioned the stool. Without a word she set herself up for a massé, the most difficult shot in the game. The cue-ball had to be hit off-centre with a downward thrust which spun it so viciously that instead of shooting off in a straight line, the ball executed a violent swerve, thus taking it around the intermediary ball and striking the target ball.

'Hold on there,' Bill protested, suddenly very serious. 'What kind of shot do you think you're going to play?'

Judy looked at him without a flicker of uncertainty. 'I'm going to attempt a massé so as to pot the red in the centre pocket.'

'A massé!' he squeaked.

Larry burst out laughing. 'A massé, for God's sake! You've been watching too much television, my little fairy. Only a champion can hope to play that with any success.'

'And there goes my cloth if you miss,' Bill added feelingly.

'Hey, Judy,' Mal chimed in, his voice pitched to warm reasonableness, 'I don't want to win that much.'

Judy fixed a challenging blue gaze on her host. 'If I tear the cloth I'll pay for it to be replaced. All right?'

He hesitated and his wife purred into the moment of indecision, 'Darling, you can't possibly refuse that offer. Besides, you couldn't deprive us of this delightful entertainment.'

Bill Holgate was not amused. He shot his wife a baleful look, then tight-lipped with disapproval he nevertheless nodded his permission. 'As you like.'

'Judy . . .' Mal began, frowning hard.

She silenced him with a stabbing look and set herself again for the shot. The atmosphere around the table was tense with expectancy. It reacted on Judy like a spurt of adrenalin. She was not confident of making the shot but she was intent on making a damned good attempt.

With intense concentration and a heightened sense of drama she struck the cue-ball. Too hard. The instant after-judgement brought a sick disappointment. Then the vicious spin suddenly took effect. She watched in growing glee as the cue-ball swerved back around the blue and soundly tapped the red. There was a sharp intake of breath around the table as the red ball rolled into the side-pocket.

'Holy shit! She's done it!' Larry Davis gasped in stunned disbelief.

Judy flashed him a glance which barely concealed her contempt. She picked up her stool. As she walked around to the other side of the table for the next shot, everyone stepped back out of her way. She enjoyed the mixture of expressions on their faces; chagrin on Vivien's, amazement and relief on Bill's, undisguised delight on Ruth's, amusement on Patrick's, and not quite so much boredom on Felicity's. Judy made a point of not looking at Mal. She was determined on not caring about his reaction to anything.

The position of the cue-ball was perfect for the next shot. The game was now relatively straightforward. Taking each colour in professional style, she proceeded to pot all but one with machine-gun efficiency. The pink was jammed up hard on a side-cushion. She knew that technically she had to hit the ball and the cushion simultaneously. Its successful execution required precision and a very good table, but with all the heady confidence of a player on a hot streak, Judy took aim and struck truly. The pink ran along the cushion, teetered on the edge of the top pocket and dropped in. Patrick and Ruth Hagan applauded enthusiastically and Judy threw them a smile before sinking the black with sharp finality.

She turned to Mal with an air of innocent enquiry. 'Did we win, partner?'

He grinned. 'We sure did, little dynamo.'

'Where in hell did a girl like you learn to play like that?' Larry burst out in a fit of male pique.

Judy threw a mocking glance at Felicity before answering. 'There are advantages in attending a local school. By living at home I had the opportunity to learn from my father who was amateur champion of the state for many years. Oh, and by the way, Bill . . .' she turned to him with a sweet smile of condescension, '. . . I congratulate you on your table. It's true championship quality.'

His mouth quirked in amusement. 'That's very kind of you. And thank you for the delightful entertainment,' he added with a sardonic glace at his wife.

He was a good sport. Judy's smile became more genuine before she recomposed her face into cool determination. 'And now, Mal, I want to go home. It's late and I'm a working girl.'

She was all pumped up to fight if he made any

demur to her demand. The evening up to this point had been a defeat in every emotional sense and she was going to leave on a note of triumph, however empty the triumph was. Either Mal sensed her adamant purpose or was quite willing to leave anyway.

'Well, anything after that performance would be an anti-climax,' he grinned. 'Bill, Viv, thanks for the evening. We will not linger.'

There was a short delay while goodbyes were effected. Judy was pleasantly surprised by Ruth Hagan's warm hand-clasp and even more surprised by her words, 'Good luck, Judy. I hope you win.'

Win what? she wondered, then shrugged off her puzzlement. She was going home, away from these people, and she did not expect to ever meet them again. Vivien prolonged their departure by hanging on to Mal and giving him a kiss which could only be classified as a hostess special. Judy grimaced in disgust and walked ahead to the car. To hell with them, she thought angrily. They can play their games without her as a bystander.

Mal beat her to the passenger-door. She thanked him politely as she settled into the seat. Good manners and dignity to the bitter end, she decided, coldly ignoring him while he settled himself and put the car in motion.

'That was a fantastic show of skill, Judy,' he commented admiringly. 'Forgive me for doubting you?'

The familiar tease in his voice made her bridle. 'You weren't to know,' she replied shortly.

'If your father taught you, he must be good enough to be a professional.'

'Yes. He could've been.'

'Why didn't he have a crack at it? There's big money in snooker.'

'It would've meant travelling.'

'So?'

Judy sighed. Malcolm Stewart would never sympathise with the sentiments which had kept her father at home to share the responsibility of Billy. 'He didn't want to travel.'

'Why not?'

His puzzlement irked her. 'Some men consider their family life more important than chasing personal stardom,' she said with pointed irony.

'But surely your family could have shared in his success,' he argued.

'You wouldn't understand,' she muttered.

'Why wouldn't I understand?'

In a flash of irritation she snapped, 'Because you come first with you, and you wouldn't care whom you hurt to get your own way.'

There was a sharp intake of breath and a short, tense silence. Judy could feel his eyes on her but she stared straight ahead, fiercely wishing that the short drive to his house was over.

'That's a pretty harsh judgement, Judy. I don't like it and I don't think it's true,' he stated with slow deliberation. 'What have I said or done to give you such an impression?'

She bit her lips, annoyed with herself for having revealed her inner resentment.

'I thought I'd explained why I didn't tell you my name. Are you still holding a grudge against me for that little deception?'

She shook her head, not wanting to say any more.

'But you're upset about something. Tell me,' he persisted.

She kept a stony silence.

'Judy . . .' He felt for her hand.

She repulsed his attempt at physical contact, shuddering at the mere thought of letting him touch her.

Hey! What's wrong?' he protested.

'I just want to go home,' she declared stubbornly and folded her arms in an emphatic rejection of any friendly overture.

He sighed in exasperation and pressed his foot on the accelerator. He drove with insolent speed and to Judy's relief they arrived in the gravelled courtyard without accident and without further conversation. She did not wait for him to open her door. She stepped out of the car while he was still on his way. She offered him a polite handshake which he ignored.

'Thank you for an evening which was instructive rather than pleasant,' she said coolly. 'If you want more turf I'll see that someone else delivers it. Goodbye and better luck next time.'

The concern on his face stiffened into anger. 'What the hell does that mean?'

She stepped around him, giving a blithe little wave as she passed. 'It means thanks for the memory. Ta-ta to little Judy.'

He caught her hand in a punishing grip, forcing her to a halt.

'That hand is mine,' she said pointedly, facing him with haughty disdain.

'You can have it back after I've got some sense out of you,' he said with grim determination.

She relaxed and gave him a saccharin smile.

'Oh, do let's retain our sense of humour, Mal! Isn't that what you love about me?'

'I don't find this particularly humorous. I thought we had something going between us.'

'Ah, but that was before I realised I was a second-class substitute for Vivien Holgate,' Judy said airily.

'A what?'

'You know. A sort of understudy. Not quite the star but someone who'll do to fill in. Might even satisfy the audience, too. I do hope you were pleased with me, Mal. Particularly since you underwrote the expense of fitting me for the part. But I'm not star-quality and I find the part distasteful. I'll post you a cheque to cover your losses. Felicity gave me a good idea of how much I owe you. Just let go my hand and wave me good-bye.'

'The dress! The goddamned dress!' he groaned. 'Judy, the money meant nothing to me. I just wanted you to feel happy and I thought you might baulk at the price.'

'So you took the decision out of my hands. How very kind and thoughtful of you! I don't suppose it had anything to do with your getting your own way.'

'That, too, I suppose,' he admitted grudgingly. 'I didn't want you to have a reason for not coming with me tonight.'

'Oh yes, that's right,' Judy mocked. 'You wanted me with you so that everyone would be convinced that you had a mistress who was not Vivien Holgate. All those casual little remarks dropped here and there that I would be going no further than your house tonight. Well, lover, you assumed too damned much. I do not appreciate being marked in public as anyone's mistress. Particularly when I'm not. So you can sleep with that thought!'

'Do you think anyone cared?' he cried in frustration and dropped her hand to lift both of his in appeal. 'For God's sake! No one questions who's sleeping with whom these days. They don't care!'

'I care. And I'm very choosy about whom I sleep with.' She enunciated the words with icy precision.

'You weren't so damned cool towards me this afternoon. If Viv hadn't interrupted . . .'

'But she did. And one can forgive oneself a mistake now and then,' Judy added loftily, taking advantage of her freedom to step past him and stride towards her car.

'I'm not finished with you,' came the exasperated mutter. He grabbed hold of her shoulder and swung her back again. This time he gripped her upper arms, fingers digging angrily into the soft flesh.

She stared him straight in the eye. 'To use your superior strength to hold me against my will, earns my utmost contempt.'

'My God! You're an impossible woman!'

'You said it. Impossible. So let me go.'

He heaved a feeling sigh and loosened his grip. 'All right! All right! I shouldn't have lied about the price of the dress and I shouldn't have suggested that we were lovers. I'm sorry I hurt your pride. I'm sorry I was indiscreet. And whatever idea you've got about me and Viv Holgate is wrong. Now . . .' his hands slid down her arms to take a light hold of her fingers, '. . . can we go inside, sit down, have a civilised drink and sort this all out?'

'No, thank you. I want to go home. I've had quite enough of being civilised tonight.' And she wouldn't believe him whatever he said. She had seen that quick understanding between him and Vivien Holgate with her own eyes. An intimate understanding.

'Judy ... Judy ...' he breathed in soft appeal, moving closer and drawing her into an embrace.

She steeled herself to unrelenting stiffness. 'I hope you're only contemplating a good night kiss,' she said flippantly. 'I'll suffer that if I have to.'

'Happy suffering,' he murmured and took possession of her mouth before she could close it.

He worked hard at getting a response. Judy had to admire his technique. He was a damned good lover with his seductive mouth and caressing hands. She could have stayed switched off mentally. All she had to do was keep thinking of Vivien Holgate. But temptation whispered that this was the last time she would experience the sensual exhilaration of his lovemaking ... and a kiss wouldn't hurt ... just one goodbye kiss. So she gave in to his persuasion and her sudden response triggered an outpouring of passion which well-nigh welded them together.

Holy smoke! Judy thought, and it was her last coherent thought for some time. Her body spoke its own language and the only word it thrummed was yes, yes, yes. It was only when Mal broke off his onslaught of kisses to murmur, 'Let's go inside', that her mind clicked back into working order.

'No thanks. You're a good kisser, Mal, I'd have to concede that,' she prattled out dizzily, struggling to sober up fast. 'That was a sizzling goodbye. A winner all the way. Only I've got this

built-in conditioner, and it says the only future in
going inside with you is occupying your bed, and
I have another future mapped out for myself.'

'Like what?' he demanded tightly.

'Like loving a man who's not just using my
body as a convenience to work off his sexual
frustration. A man who cares about my feelings.'

'I care, dammit!' he exploded.

'Then prove it by letting me go, because I want
to go home,' Judy stated with relentless logic.

He sucked in a long breath and let it out
slowly. 'I can't win, can I? No matter what I do
or say, I can't win.'

'That's about it,' Judy agreed. 'I'm the original
impossible woman. You're well rid of me.'

He nodded a couple of times then threw up his
hands in defeat. 'You want to go? Go. Leave me.
Get in your car and drive home. You're right.
You're absolutely right. You're not only impossible, you're completely bloody-minded, and I
learnt long ago that beating one's head against a
brick wall only produces one hell of a headache.
You are free to go. I even hope you find your
smugly mapped-out future. Good night, goodbye,
and fare thee well, Daisy Mae. It was fun
knowing you before you turned into strait-
laced Judith.'

The blood drained from Judy's face. It was
what she had imagined he would say to her, and
she had asked for it, but it still hurt. Unbearably.
'Goodbye,' she whispered, and with head down
and legs working to insistent orders, she walked
over to the Commodore and seated herself behind
the wheel.

With trembling fingers she forced the key into
the ignition, turned it. Her foot pressed the

accelerator with mindless force. The car jarred
into reverse, spraying gravel everywhere. Tears
blinded her eyes as she braked and pushed the
gear into drive. Another burst of gravel and she
was off, careering down the driveway, skidding
through the left hand turn on to the road,
speeding away. Away from him. Away from . . .
oh, God! Why couldn't it have been different?

CHAPTER SIX

'How was the party last night?'

Judy had been expecting the enquiry all through breakfast. Her mother was always interested in hearing the details of any social activities. This morning it had seemed that Judy might escape the usual quiz. Billy had left the table and she was just finishing her coffee when the question came. As far as Judy was concerned the party and Malcolm Stewart formed a closed book and she did not want to leaf through its pages.

Deliberately affecting a nonchalant air she turned to her mother, intending to shrug it all away. Tess Campbell's large blue eyes were bright with expectancy. Judy had inherited much from her mother, her petite figure, the small face which the years had fleshed out to plumpness, the thick curly hair, its fairness dulling into grey. The age-lines on her face were a mixture of grief and happiness. Life had not been easy with Billy but Tess Campbell's nature was optimistic and the contentment in her marriage was written on her face.

Judy gave a dismissive smile. 'Not my kind of people, Mum. It was a mistake going.'

Disappointment clouded the brightness. 'Oh! What a shame! And you looked so lovely in your new dress.'

Judy grimaced at the thought of how much of her savings had to be withdrawn to pay for the wretched dress.

'Thought you'd found yourself a man you fancied,' her father remarked questioningly.

'Yeah ... well ... that was a mistake, too,' Judy said glumly, then brightened, 'But I cleaned them up at snooker, Dad. Even pulled off a massé. You would have been proud of me.'

'No kidding! Tell me all about it. Bet they were surprised.'

She quite enjoyed recounting her little triumph and her father's warm approval and delighted comments lifted her spirits. They grinned at each other in perfect understanding.

Tess Campbell sighed. 'Judy, I've warned you about beating men at games. They don't like it. Drew, you shouldn't encourage her.'

'Nonsense! What's a game in the overall pattern of things?' he protested laughingly. 'Would you have our daughter deny her natural talents?'

Tess Campbell shook her head. 'They still don't like it.'

'Not to worry, Mum. Those people didn't mean anything to me,' Judy assured her. It was a lie. Malcolm Stewart had meant a great deal to her, but if she kept telling herself the lie, maybe it would soon become the truth.

'Besides, any man worth having wouldn't want Judy to hide her light under a bushel of pretence,' Drew Campbell declared. 'She's as good as a man any day. Better even. Aren't you, Judy?'

'You said it, Dad,' she agreed breezily.

'But she's not a man, Drew,' her mother pointed out with a frown of impatience. 'And it's time you stopped encouraging her to be one. Here she is in a man's profession, doing a man's work, and ... and ... I want her to get married and have a woman's life,' she finished limply.

The halting plea produced a prickly silence.

'I've only ever encouraged Judy to do what she wants to do, Tess. Which is her right as an individual,' came the slow, measured reply.

Judy jumped to her feet and gave her mother an affectionate hug. 'Don't you worry, Mum. One day I'll find some gorgeous man and bowl him over. Married in no time.'

Her mother sighed and gave a wry little smile. 'That's just what you would do, Judy. Bowl him over. Oh, don't mind me. Your father's right. As usual. It was just that you looked so beautiful last night and I hoped ... well, never mind. You're still young.'

'That's right. Someone even thought I was still a schoolgirl last night.'

'Naturally you corrected him,' her mother said drily, rolling her eyes up at Judy. 'Men don't like being corrected either.'

Judy grinned. 'It was a her.' She dropped a kiss on her mother's forehead and skipped out of the kitchen before anything more could be said.

She knew there was wisdom in her mother's words but there was truth in her father's. Her mother's way might catch a man but Judy did not want a relationship in which she always had to play second. Mal had not seemed to resent her skill last night. And he had not minded her correcting him about the tree. She was sure ...

Her lips thinned in self-disgust. There was no point whatsoever in thinking about Malcolm Stewart. That was over. Finished. And it wouldn't have led her to anything good. Quite clearly he was not a marrying man. Not even a man who concentrated on one woman at a time. There could be no expectation of happiness with him. She had done the right thing. Strait-laced she might be but loose living did not appeal to her. She wanted love which encompassed permanence; security, marriage, family. Reciting the words with obstinate conviction, Judy walked down to the nursery to potter around the plants.

The nursery was a good place for keeping busy. There was always something that could be done. For the next few days Judy worked like the dynamo Mal had called her, only taking the time away from it to go into town and get a bank-cheque to cover the extra cost of the dress. She sent it to him with a short, formal covering note, then shut the whole affair out of her mind.

On Wednesday night she played in the regular competition round at the local tennis club, but she was off her game. The men who partnered her in the mixed doubles egged her on to do better and she thought to herself that they didn't mind her playing well. But they weren't personally involved with her either. This man/woman thing was full of contradictions.

On Thursday her father confronted her with an order form and a teasing smile. 'Want to do another turf delivery to the same place this Saturday?'

The jolt to her heart was alarmingly strong. Urgent questions crowded her mind. Mal would have received the cheque and the cold little note which had accompanied it. Why had he rung here? There were other turf suppliers. Did he want her to come? Was he giving her a chance to change her mind? Hold it right there, she told herself sternly. Nothing had changed and she was not going to make a fool of herself.

She shook her head. 'No thanks, Dad.'

He raised his eyebrows at her vehemence. 'You were quite keen last Saturday afternoon.'

She shrugged. 'You can get Alf to do it, can't you?'

'No problem. Just thought I'd ask.'

Her father returned to the nursery office and Judy stared into blank space. The arrogance of the man to think she would turn up again! As if he only had to beckon and she would be around begging for his favours. No way! He could find himself some other Daisy Mae to fall into his lap and purr his tunes. Not Judy Campbell.

All the same, when Saturday morning came and the truck took off on its delivery run to Malcolm Stewart, Judy watched it go with mixed feelings. No matter how much she scolded herself and recited all the reasons why Malcolm Stewart was no good for her, the pang of regret in her heart could not be denied. She hoped he would not want any more turf from their nursery. It would be easier for her peace of mind if there were no more reminders of him.

Judy always spent Monday morning in the nursery office writing up the accounts. She was busily checking over the orders from a florist when the guttural clearing of a throat announced a customer at the door. She looked up into a pair of dancing green eyes.

Malcolm Stewart was leaning against the door-jamb as if he had been watching her for some time. Judy was immediately conscious that her appearance was short of best. She tended to pull at her hair when concentrating on office-work and the checked shirt and jeans were well-worn and not exactly fashionable. In sharp contrast, Mal looked the picture of sartorial elegance in a well-tailored business suit. Executive class. And sickeningly handsome. Judy simply stared at him, too dazed to gather her wits.

He wriggled his fingers at her and gave a hopeful smile as if he wasn't quite sure of a favourable reception. 'Busy?'

She covered her inner agitation by putting on the welcoming smile she always used for customers. 'I'm sorry. I didn't see you arrive. Can I help you?'

'Ummm . . .' He stroked his chin as if giving the matter some thought. 'Well, let's put it this way. You can if you want to. I came to see you.'

Her heart pitter-pattered in double-quick time but she managed to keep her outward composure coolly dignified. 'Why?'

His hands lifted in a gesture of helplessness. 'I tried. I really tried. But I couldn't keep away.'

'Oh?' Judy leaned back in her chair and surveyed him with sceptical eyes. 'You've managed for . . . what's it been . . . nine days? I would've thought you had sufficient grit to keep away from an impossible woman?'

'Ah!' One finger flew up as inspiration hit. 'But you see, I got this irrepressible urge to improve my snooker game and who better to come to but a proven expert?'

Amusement tugged at the corners of her mouth but she managed to stifle the smile. 'Then I'll call my father. I'm sure he'll only be too pleased to give you lesson's. She rose to her feet, all efficient purpose.

He came forward with upraised hands. 'I've changed my mind.'

Judy's eyebrows arched in mock surprise. 'So quickly?'

'What I really came about is trees,' he declared smugly. 'I know you're a tree specialist.'

She couldn't help it. The laughter bubbled out of her throat before she could stop it.

Mal hitched himself on to the front edge of her desk and grinned his satisfaction. 'I thought you might come with the turf on Saturday. When you didn't I said to myself, Mal, this woman means business. So business it is.'

'Business,' Judy echoed weakly and subsided back into her chair.

'Uh-huh. Looks like you've got a prosperous business here. All those igloo hot-houses, turf-farming, ferneries . . .'

'But you've come about trees,' Judy reminded him sardonically.

The mobile eyebrows reproved her interruption with their now familiar jiggle. 'Well, not exactly trees. Trees are only a part of it. But I'm sure you'll agree they're very important. Of course there are other things like shrubs, the occasional flower, maybe even a vegetable or two. I'm very fond of fresh spinach. Do you like spinach?'

'If it's cooked properly.'

'Ah yes! A bit of water, salt and pepper, a dob of butter and a squeeze of lemon juice.' He smacked his lips. 'Nothing like it. I'm a very good cook. How about I cook dinner for you tonight?'

Her smile died. Dinner, bed and breakfast more likely. 'No. No, thank you,' she said sharply. Her lashes swept down, an instinctive defence against his probing gaze.

'Judy, I am not the wicked wolf of the west

who gobbles up little girls for supper,' he said with quiet force.

She took a deep, calming breath and produced a light banter. 'Oh, I'd be bound to stick in your throat anyway. Little girls aren't as tender as they look and this one didn't come down in the last shower either. The answer is still no.'

'Even to a business dinner?'

She flicked a glance at him. His expression had the confidence of a man who had the trump card up his sleeve. 'We have no business to discuss,' she stated evenly.

'Now there you're wrong. You see, I had this idea that if you came over to my house . . . say about six o'clock this evening . . . we could walk over the grounds and I could cook dinner while you look over the surveyor's contour map and the scale map of the block with its exact positioning of the house and pool and tennis-court, etcetera . . .' He paused to draw breath and a little smile played on his lips. 'And then we could eat dinner while we discuss how much it's going to cost me for you to design and carry through all the landscaping.'

Judy repressed the instant well of excitement, not daring to believe him. The large blue eyes lifted to his in an agony of doubt. 'Mal, don't kid me. Not on something like this.'

He looked astonished. 'Would I kid you? What do you think I am? Stupid? You kissed me goodbye for a couple of harmless little deceptions. I'd be plumb crazy to try one on this scale.'

Her face lit up like a Christmas tree. 'You mean it. You really mean it.'

'I do.'

She jumped to her feet and rushed around the

desk to him, bubbling with sheer exhilaration. 'Oh, Mal! You wonderful, wonderful man! I'll do a great job. The very best. I ached to do the landscaping as soon as I saw the house. I know I can make it a real show-place. You won't regret giving me this chance. I'm good, you know. I won prizes at college. Oh, thank you for coming to me!'

Impulsively she took his hands and squeezed them in an excess of gratitude. Mal slid from the perch on the desk and suddenly her hands were on his chest and his hands were gliding around her back. The green eyes danced down at her, lovely, sparkling green eyes which shared her excitement and promised more.

'Let's hear the wonderful man part again. I liked the sound of that,' he softly teased.

Her heart was bursting with so much positive emotion it was quite impossible to switch into negative. Indeed, Judy did not even consider it. In fact, her mouth was still curved into an ecstatic smile when his mouth grazed over it, igniting a whole burst of positive signals which impelled her to fling her arms around his neck and meet his kiss with one of her own. Happiness and excitement lent fervour to her impulse, then welded into something else entirely. A great welling of love melted her bones and sent a glorious, tingling warmth all around her body, right to her fingertips.

'I hope you don't kiss every customer like that, my girl,' Mal breathed as he came up for air.

'You caught me in a moment of weakness,' Judy said shakily.

'May there be many of them. I could live with that kind of weakness,' he muttered and kissed her again before Judy had a chance to recover her equilibrium.

'Aar-rhum!'

Judy tore her mouth away from Mal's and with her heart hammering a protest at the abrupt parting, she turned startled eyes towards the door. Her father stood there, his weathered face a picture of amazement and curiosity.

'I apologise for interrupting something so ... umm ... personal, but your mother's ready to take the mail, Judy. Is it done?'

Mail, she thought distractedly, and finally found voice. 'Yes ... yes ... it's here.' She swivelled out of Mal's embrace and snatched up the envelopes from the desk. A flush of embarrassment burnt her cheeks as she swung around to hand them to her father. She could not bring herself to look him in the eye. 'Oh, Dad, this is Malcolm Campbell ... I mean Stewart ... Malcolm Stewart. Mal, this is my father, Drew Campbell.'

Well, she had made a right mess of that. Take a hold of yourself, my girl, Judy counselled herself sternly. Mal was grinning from ear to ear as he stepped over to offer a hand to her father.

'A pleasure to meet you, Mr Campbell,' he said with ringing conviction. 'Judy and I were just settling some business.'

Drew Campbell cast a measuring eye over Mal as he took the hand. The two men were much the same height and build. Despite his iron-grey hair and fifty years of age, Judy's father still had the look of an athlete, back straight, loose-limbed, leanly muscled, and with a steadiness of eye which could quickly sort out a man of less forcefulness of character.

'Business,' he echoed with dry emphasis. 'I take it you've met my daughter before today, Mr Stewart.'

Mal chuckled and threw Judy a teasing look. 'We had something of a misunderstanding last Saturday, and I've been trying to convince Judy that I really am a man of my word.'

'Here's the mail, Dad.' Judy thrust the bundle of envelopes at him, hoping he would take the hint and go.

He shuffled the envelopes with the casual air of a man in no hurry to leave. 'Malcolm Stewart, eh? Good Scottish name. Seem to have heard it recently in connection with something or other. Let me see now . . .'

Judy leapt in impatiently. 'He's the architect who designed the Fairway Tourist Centre.'

'Ah, yes!' Her father nodded a couple of times. 'And you'd be the man who helped Judy with the turf last week.'

'That's right,' Mal agreed cheerfully.

Judy gritted her teeth. The inquisition had to stop. It was getting too embarrassing. 'Dad! I thought Mum was waiting for the mail.'

'So she is. Must be on my way. Interesting to meet you, Mr Stewart.' He was almost out of the door when he stopped and looked back. 'Oh, one little point of idle curiosity,' he said blandly. 'Do you play snooker, Mr Stewart?'

Judy rolled her eyes back in exasperation.

Mal grinned. 'Yes, I do, but not as skilfully as your daughter.'

Drew Campbell smiled. 'Good, isn't she? Taught her myself. I'd be happy to give you some lessons if you ever feel the need to beat her. Be seeing you, Mr Stewart.'

Judy sagged back against the desk and covered her burning face with her hands. Mal forcibly peeled them away but she refused to open her eyes and look at him.

'I'm sorry about that,' she mumbled in intense mortification. 'My father is . . .'

'A very astute man.'

She sighed and raised her lashes a little, still uncertain of Mal's reaction despite his amused tone. 'I was going to say a terrible tease.'

'His daughter is very like him.'

The low murmur warned her that his mouth was coming closer. Her lashes flew up and she snatched her hand from his to whip it between them.

'Oh no! Not again. You're not to kiss me again, Malcolm Stewart. This is business, remember?'

He rocked back on his heels, eyeing her with twinkling amusement. 'I know you'll correct me if I'm wrong, but I had the distinct impression that you were kissing me a few moments ago.'

'That was gratitude,' she insisted hotly.

'Gratitude,' he mocked. 'Sure that's all it was?'

'Absolutely. You'd just handed me the kind of showcase for my talents that I've dreamed about. I can see it now. Architect: Malcolm Stewart. Landscaper: Judith Campbell. I'll bring my signboard with me tonight and nail it under yours. Great advertisement.'

His eyes glittered with provocative mischief. 'So, now you only want me for my name.' He sighed and lifted his hands in mock despair. 'I knew it would come to this. That's why I preferred to be nameless. Last Saturday we had a pure attraction between us, unsullied by . . .'

'Pure!'

'Don't interrupt. I've got a full head of steam. As I said, a pure attraction. And you can't deny it because that kind of thing is not one-sided. Then I tell you my name and bingo! I get accused of all sorts of villainy and here you are, getting ready to commercialise our relationship.'

'The only relationship we have is a business relationship,' Judy retorted hotly.

'And whose fault is that?'

Judy stamped her foot in frustration. 'Will you stop this?'

'Stop what? I'm only stating the truth. I thought you were a stickler for the truth, Judy.'

She put her hands on her hips and glowered at him. 'The truth is, I'm not in the market for the position of Malcolm Stewart's mistress, but I am in the market for landscaping. Now, are you, or are you not, offering me a business proposition, because that's all I'm interested in.'

He shook his head in mock reproof. 'Such a sexist word, mistress. I wouldn't dream of demeaning a woman I like by asking her to be my mistress. Friend, companion, lover . . . that's another matter . . . whatever is mutually desirable. I'm all for equal rights and equal responsibility. Women's lib is the best thing that ever happened to men.'

He sighed and gave a careless shrug. 'However, I digress from the burning question. Yes, I am offering you the landscaping.' He glanced down at his watch. 'I have half an hour before I must leave for a meeting at Fairway. Why don't you show me around the nursery? Be completely businesslike . . . since that's what you want,' he added with a sly little smile which tested her composure to the limit.

Giving him a tour of the nursery was a better idea than staying here in the office with him. He had stirred a tumult of emotional confusion and she needed a blast of fresh air to clear her head. 'All right,' she said in a tightly firm voice. 'Let's go.'

No sooner were they out the door when he caught her hand and held it prisoner in his. A warm tingle danced up her arm and she tried to pull away, wary of encouraging any physical contact. He ignored her effort and retained possession.

'Lovely day, isn't it?' he said pleasantly.

After a brief fight with herself Judy gave up. Holding hands was a harmless enough activity and she liked the feel of his fingers around hers. It was nice and friendly. And he was giving her the landscape job. 'Yes. It's a lovely, lovely day,' she agreed, her spirits lifting once again in heady excitement.

He grinned down at her. She smiled back. He was a lovely, lovely man, even though he didn't believe in marriage. And he was giving her the chance to make a name for herself. It was all she could do to stop her feet from skipping along. Ideas for the landscaping started zinging through her mind and it was difficult to concentrate even part of her thoughts to explaining the operation of the nursery.

'As you can see, the flats near the creek are used for turf-farming. All our irrigation comes from the creek except in times of severe drought when we switch over to the big dam. The field beyond the hot-houses is planted with carnations. This is the most commercially viable flower. We also grow orchids and speciality flowers like stephanotis for ... for bridal bouquets.'

Mal arched an eyebrow at her. 'Well, that's certainly a viable market with most people getting married two or three times these days.' A deep scepticism crept into his voice. 'Just a bloody side-show, weddings. Sweet-smelling flowers on the day and divorce behind the door. But I daresay it's good business for those who supply the trappings.'

'Yes. Funerals are good too,' she bit out sharply. 'And births,' she added for good measure. Let him scoff at those, she thought resentfully, then chided herself for being un-reasonable. Mal was a product of a broken marriage and probably had deep-rooted reasons for his scepticism. But there was an odd, sinking feeling in her heart.

She led him through the hot-houses. 'Each igloo is for indoor plants at different stages of growth. The mature plants command a very good price at florists and supermarkets. A lot of people want instant interior decoration and are prepared to pay handsomely for advanced plants.'

Mal browsed around, admiring some of the more unusual varieties of foliage which were on display, asking questions and showing a keen interest in her answers. Judy became more and more animated, fired by an inner elation which she did not stop to question. Never had she enjoyed showing off her knowledge so much and the warm admiration in the green eyes was positively intoxicating.

Finally they came to the ferneries. Billy was in the potting section, transferring some of the larger ferns into hanging baskets, ready for sale.

He turned to Judy with an eager smile but as soon as he saw Mal he ducked his head back down and performed a sideways shuffle which spoke all too eloquently of discomfort. It wrenched Judy's heart. Billy had learnt to expect rejection from strangers. Suddenly it was very important to her to test Mal's reaction to her brother.

'How are you going there, Billy?' she asked brightly.

He gave her a furtive, anxious look. 'All right. Dad said for me to do those. I'm almost finished.'

'You're doing a good job.' She smiled to allay his anxiety. 'This is a friend of mine, Malcolm Stewart.'

Billy turned around slowly, darting a shy glance at Mal while nervously rubbing his dirty hands on his jeans. 'Hello, Mr . . . um . . .' A frantic look at Judy.

She tensed, despite her intention to act naturally.

'Why don't you call me Mal?'

The easy grin and the outstretched hand settled Billy's uncertainty. A smile of boyish delight lit his face. 'All right. Pleased to meet you, Mal.' He thrust out an eager hand, realised it was dirty and began to withdraw it in dismay.

Mal caught it and gave a friendly handshake. 'You've got a nice place to work, Billy. Not too many men as lucky as you.' There was no note of condescension, just straightforward statement of appreciation for the pleasant environment of massed ferns.

'Yes. I'm lucky,' Billy agreed joyously. 'I like ferns. I like driving the tractor, too. I'm going to drive it when I finish this job.'

'Well, we'd better not keep you from your work then. It's a great day for driving tractors.'

'Yes. Great day,' Billy echoed, happiness beaming from the big smile and the innocent blue eyes.

'I'm showing Mal around. See you later, Billy,' Judy said with an answering smile.

'See you. See you, Mal.'

He gave Billy a jaunty salute. Billy laughed and saluted back. Judy's hand was given a gentle squeeze as they walked back outside and she felt such a flood of relief and gratitude that she could not speak, could not even look at him. Few people had ever accepted Billy so naturally on first meeting and she had given Mal no warning.

'Was your brother born with brain damage?'

The question was matter-of-fact and she managed to match his tone. 'No. He almost died from meningitis when he was a child. As you can see, he's still a child.'

'How old is he now?'

'Nineteen.'

'With a mental age of?'

'Eight.'

'And how old are you, Judy?'

'Twenty-two.' She had answered automatically and only in the ensuing silence did she wonder why he had asked her age at that particular moment. 'What's my age got to do with my brother?'

'Nothing.' He smiled at her puzzled frown. 'Just working out a few things.'

'Like what?'

'Like why you're so aggressively independent.' He glanced at his watch. 'Much as I hate to leave you, it's time for me to go.' He turned her towards him and brushed her cheek with his knuckles. 'Six o'clock this evening?'

'I'll be there,' she promised. 'And thanks again, Mal.'

He grinned and the green eyes danced with devilment. 'Keep the gratitude burning bright. It seems to be a softening agent.'

She tried to look stern. 'It's strictly business, remember?'

'Would I dare suggest anything else?'

He was off before she could contradict him, striding purposefully towards his car with the confident air of a man who would dare anything. The Aston Martin started with a roar. An exciting, dashing car, not by any stretch of the imagination, a family car. Just like the man.

She wished . . . ah well! No point in wishing for the moon. After all, she had been given the chance to reach the stars, a landscape contract which could start off the reputation she hoped to build. If she made a stunning success of landscaping Malcolm Stewart's property, then maybe other people in the new estate would seek her out. And once the ball started rolling . . .

'Going to day-dream for the rest of the day?'

Judy whirled around to find her father emerging from one of the ferneries. 'Oh, Dad! I've got a job. A big, lovely contract!'

'Well, well, what do you know? I don't suppose it'd be Mr Stewart's house?'

'Yes. Isn't it marvellous?'

'Marvellous! I'm very happy for you. And there you were, thinking that your femininity was a handicap. They do say that the way to a man's heart is through his stomach. Rot, of course! However, I wonder if Mr Stewart figures that the

way to a woman's heart is through her landscaping.'

'Dad!' she said in an admonishing tone. 'It's
not like that at all.'

'Oh, I forgot. All contracts are sealed with a
kiss nowadays. Handshakes are old-fashioned,
aren't they?'

'It won't happen again. He just caught me by
surprise. It's strictly business. I told him so.'

'Well, love,' the blue eyes twinkled with
suppressed laughter, 'I wouldn't count on him
staying told. He looked as if he was the kind of a
man who had a mind of his own. Still, that's your
business and good luck to you.'

She sighed and gave her father a wry look. 'No
good, Dad. He'll have to stay told. He's not a
marrying man.'

Her father took her arm and tucked it into his.
He patted her hand in an indulgent way as he
walked her towards the house. 'I seem to
remember saying something like that to your
mother a long time ago. Funny how a woman can
change a man's mind. He starts doing all sorts of
things, going right out of his way, just to please
her. Quite extraordinary!'

'You're an old romantic,' she chided him, and
embarrassed by his interest, Judy started de-
scribing the kind of social life Malcolm Stewart
led.

But her father's words came back to her later.
When she was alone. She wondered, with a
growing degree of pleasure, if she had judged
Malcolm Stewart too harshly.

CHAPTER SEVEN

JUDY did not bring her signboard with her. Exuberance had simmered down to a cautious level. No contract had yet been signed in black and white. Even the verbal agreement had only encompassed a design and costing operation. Until Mal gave his approval of her plans it would be decidedly premature to nail her signboard under his.

All afternoon she had been sketching out ideas to show him. Now as she turned into his driveway she braked the Commodore to a halt and let her gaze roam over the grounds. The gleam of possession was in her eyes as she visualised what was, as yet, only on paper. The trees in her imagination stood proud and tall against a background of native shrubs. Excitement stirred her blood and she drove up to the house with a spurt of acceleration.

With her folder of sketches under her arm Judy tried to adopt a business-like air. The urge to be feminine had warred against practicality and she had topped her neat denim skirt with a peasant-style blouse of fine, white lawn which was prettily embroidered around neckline and sleeves. After much hesitation she had left her hair loose. A hard brushing had reduced the unruly curls to a semblance of order.

The only concession she had really made to business was the joggers on her feet. Sandals were simply not suitable for walking over rough ground. And after all, she did not want Mal thinking that this was a dinner-date. Because it wasn't. Not really. She pressed his doorbell and hugged the folder of sketches, using it as protective armour against the uncontrollable weakness in her heart.

The front door opened. Mal's expression of undiluted pleasure caused a rush of uncoordinated signals from her heart, warm blood crashing into the capillary network of her cheeks, flooding every cool bit of calculation from her brain and raising her physical awareness to an unprecedented level. She vaguely knew that her own expression mirrored his, and in that totally unguarded moment something incredibly intimate leapt between them, an intuitive recognition which all the words in the world could not describe or deny.

'I've been waiting for you,' he said in a deep mellow voice which seemed to vibrate through her whole body.

I've been waiting for you all my life, her mind sang in reply, but the harmony tripped on a jagged note of caution. Emotional commitment slid into confusion. It was too soon, too silly, too short-sighted to surrender her independence to a man who was still so much of a question mark in so many ways. She frowned and glanced at her watch, more to cover her mental retreat from him than to check the time.

'It's only just gone six o'clock,' she said, her voice sounding oddly high-pitched and squeaky. She swallowed hard and looked up at him, blue eyes now snapping with wariness.

His smile remained warm and welcoming. 'I know. I'm not usually a clock-watcher but it seems a hell of a long time since I had you to myself. Can I take that folder for you?'

'No. No, thank you,' she stammered out, hugging the folder even more tightly. What did he mean . . . to himself? Judy suspected that he was referring to that first day when they had so very nearly become lovers and she felt acutely vulnerable as she stepped inside his house. 'I brought along some preliminary sketches of ideas which you might find interesting,' she said briskly.

The attempt to lift this meeting on to a less personal footing was ignored. 'I'm glad you've been thinking of me,' he remarked. The amused glint in the green eyes was unashamedly provocative. 'I'd feel it was grossly unfair if I wasn't occupying your mind in the same distracting manner as you've occupied mine.'

She gave him a sceptical look as they reached the head of the stairs. 'I've been thinking of how to transform your land, not you.'

'Thank God for that! You like me as I am,' he retorted lightly.

He took her elbow to steer her down to the living room. Judy held her tongue, unwilling to be drawn into flirtatious banter which would be sure to undermine her purpose in being here. The landscaping was too important to be cast into second place by an attraction which was altogether too sexual. Mal led her into the kitchen.

'You can spread out your sketches on the island work-bench while I pour us a drink,' he suggested happily.

'I thought you were cooking.'

'All prepared.' His eyes twinkled with mischief. 'Used to be a boy scout.'

Judy could not help smiling. 'I can just see you singing your heart out around a camp-fire.'

'Yodelling. I was a fantastic yodeller. Want to hear me?'

'Next time we're on top of a mountain. Meanwhile I have these sketches . . .'

'Ah yes! Trees.'

'And shrubs and the occasional flower. Even a vegetable-patch for your spinach,' she added drily.

'A woman after my own heart,' he said with mock gravity. 'Unleash them from your folder. I'll uncork the champagne.'

'Champagne?'

'All contracts have to be toasted in champagne. The crowning touch of good will to legality.'

He was already taking a bottle out of the refrigerator and July decided not to quibble over a drink or two. The island-bench was clear except for small bowls of Macadamia nuts and stuffed olives. She untied her folder and set out the sketches for Mal's perusal.

'Obviously I haven't been able to do these exactly to scale but I had a fair idea of the spaces involved. You'll be able to see if a design developed along these lines will appeal to you. These sketches are more a basis for discussion than a finalised design. You probably have some ideas of your own which you'll want incorporated.'

'Nope. I have a completely open mind.' He flashed a grin at her as he finished topping up a glass. 'It's your baby all the way.'

Judy quelled her inner elation and spoke cautiously. 'It could be a very expensive baby.'

'Didn't expect otherwise,' he answered blithely,

passing her a brimming glass, then clicking it lightly with his. 'May it give us both a great deal of pleasure.'

They drank and the tingle in Judy's blood had nothing to do with champagne. Baby . . . pleasure . . . the words evoked images which could not be suppressed and Judy could feel herself flushing again under the suggestive warmth of the teasing green eyes. She was relieved when his gaze dropped to the sketches on the bench.

'What have we here? A straight gravel driveway?'

'Yes. It has to be straight or it would detract from the beautiful symmetry of the roof-line. And it has to be gravel to link it to the front courtyard. I've curved it outwards to the brick pillars so that as you drive in you get an arrow effect, highlighting the central gable. The gravel should be faced with cement, both for the aesthetic reason of colour contrast and line emphasis, and for practical reasons of good drainage and prevention of gravel dispersion to the lawn.'

He nodded. 'But the groves of trees are offset. You don't think they should continue the symmetry?'

'Too much of a good thing can kill the focal point, which is your central gable. Contrast is more artistic and the curves of the groves still lead the eye to the peak of the house.'

Confident of the artistry of her design, Judy went on to explain the purpose behind the placement of every tree and shrub. Mal kept nodding approval and she proceeded to the other sketches, detailing the kitchen garden behind the cabana, the tumbled array of bush rocks which would support specialised shrubs and greenery around the pool, the row of citrus trees which would be planted on a mound to the west of the tennis court.

'Why a mound?' Mal asked.

'Citrus trees need good drainage and your soil is mostly clay. We need to truck in rich, orchard topsoil for them to thrive, and apart from that, the mound forms an effective boundary between you and the next property. Up here . . .' she pointed to the sketch of the kitchen garden, '. . . the wire fence for the passionfruit and grape vines forms the boundary. You don't want stray dogs digging up your spinach.'

'Practical as well as brilliant.'

She glanced up to see if he was mocking her but his expression was one of sincere appreciation. 'Please say if there's anything you don't like,' she urged, a trace of doubt shadowing her enthusiasm.

'I love it. Show me more.'

He was standing next to her and she was very conscious of his closeness as she proceeded to outline the rest of her sketches. Her voice described the grouping of acacias and melaleucas for the eastern boundary, the placement of banksias, waratahs, boronias and other native flora. Behind the smooth exposition her mind was occupied with more secret thoughts, how intensely virile Mal looked in the orange body-shirt and form-hugging jeans, how electric his touch when his arm brushed against hers, how much she wanted him.

'I'm astounded that you've produced all this in a matter of hours,' he commented admiringly.

'It's been evolving in my imagination ever since I came to deliver the turf,' she admitted with a rueful little smile. 'It's the kind of place one dreams of doing but I never expected to get the opportunity. You're sure you like the concept?'

'It's fantastic!' he declared. 'And what's more, it gives me everything I could possibly want and requires very little maintenance. Let's go out and stroll around and you can point out where everything goes so I can visualise it properly.'

Dizzy with champagne and happiness Judy offered no resistance to the arm which slid around her shoulders and hugged her to his side. Mal drew her through the kitchen and laundry to the area which would become the kitchen garden.

'The vegetable plots should be built up for easy tending. It could be done in sandstone or brick, whichever you prefer,' she said, bubbling with the anticipation of turning dream into reality.

He smiled down at her. 'What do you think?'

'Brick to match the house.'

'Then brick it is.'

His absolute compliance to all her ideas was immensely gratifying and not once did it waver. When she suggested five citrus trees along the western boundary behind the tennis court he agreed that five seemed a good number. Almost as an afterthought he asked what the five should be. Judy advised lemon, mandarin, lime, valencia and navel oranges and he declared them all admirable choices. The stroll around the grounds was more satisfying than any walk Judy had taken in her entire life. They returned to the kitchen and she slowly floated back down to earth.

'Mal, you do realise all this is going to cost a great deal? The driveway alone will run to six or seven thousand.'

'Uh-huh. As I recall, the recommended expenditure for landscaping is ten to fifteen per cent of the cost of the house. I'll give you a cheque for twenty thousand dollars for starters and you can tell me when you need more,' he said as if price was no object at all.

He was pouring Judy some more champagne and she stared at him in incredulous wonder. 'Do you mean you're virtually handing me a blank cheque? You don't mind how much all this costs?'

He smiled, clearly amused by her astonishment. 'It'd be poor economy to stint on the landscaping when I've put so much into the house, and I'm sure you'll give me a full acount of all expenditure. Get the best specimens available of everything, the most advanced trees you can buy, any fertiliser you deem advisable, whatever will achieve your vision. I give you a completely free hand to carry it through to fruition.'

'Oh, Mal . . .' A huge well of emotion brought tears to her eyes. 'I can't tell you how much this means to me.'

His smile took on a faint smugness as he said, 'I think I have a fair idea.' Then he put down the bottle and looked up. His smile became stiff as he caught the luminous sheen of emotion in the large blue eyes. He frowned, made a little grimace, then sighed in exasperation. I'll write out the cheque and get the scale maps,' he muttered and strode from the room.

The curious change of expression, the roughened tone of voice and the abrupt exit had Judy wondering if she had said something wrong. Surely he could not have been irritated by her gratitude. Such a large contract would naturally inspire gratitude in anyone lucky enough to have it handed to them. With a little prickle of apprehension Judy gathered her sketches into a neat bundle and replaced them in her folder.

Several minutes passed before Mal returned. He gave her the scale maps, a cheque and a handwritten statement detailing their agreement and carrying his signature. 'Business settled,' he said with an oddly grim air.

Judy placed them in the folder but Mal's manner prompted her to ask for reassurance. 'Mal, this is what you want?'

He expelled a long breath and turned to her. The green eyes held a mocking tenderness as if he was deriding himself for feeling any softness. His hands lifted and gently cupped her face. 'Do whatever you want, Judy. If you think of anything you'd like to add to your design, add it, regardless of the cost. Give this house the kind of setting that would most please you if you were living here.'

'But it's your . . .'

The words died on her lips. He was going to kiss her. A tumult of thoughts warred across her mind. They melted into an amorphous fog and drifted away as his mouth reached hers. Such a warm, lovely mouth. Her own opened to it in instinctive response, welcoming, savouring, pleading . . . love me, please love me.

She was not aware of his hands moving from her face but suddenly her body was thrust against his and she was clinging to him, wanting, revelling in the strength which held her imprisoned. And she met his passion with all the silent craving of her heart, rapturously surren-

dering to his every demand and recklessly
inciting more.

'Judy . . .' A ragged whisper of need. A
shuddering intake of breath and then his fingers
closed tightly around hers. 'Come on . . . now.'

He was pulling her out of the kitchen, hurrying
her across the living room. Her heart was
pounding with chaotic force. Her whole body was
throbbing with a need which begged to be
appeased and her legs automatically moved to
Mal's urgency, drawn on by a power which Judy
could not deny.

Then they were in the bedroom and Mal was
undressing her with feverish haste. And she did
not care. Excitement exploded within her as he
stepped out of his clothes and there was nothing
between them. Skin grazed skin with vibrant
heat, pressed, clung, strained closer. They fell on
the bed in a whirl of frenzied passion, kissing,
grasping, owning with a fierce urgency which was
all-devouring. Sheer instinct arched her body to
meet his, wanting, inviting, shuddering with
relief at the first thrust of intimacy.

A sharp pain caught her panting breath and
held it until full penetration brought the sweet
ache of possession and a shuddering sigh of
elation. He was part of her. She was part of him.
They were one. His sudden stillness seemed
completely right to her. This was a moment to be
savoured, held, remembered, a moment of
incredible intimacy. You're mine. I'm yours. A
togetherness which had been unimaginable.

'My God!'

His words, yet they could have been hers, an
expulsion of deep emotion. Mal's breath wavered
through her hair as he lowered his head to hers.

His arms slid under her shoulders, gently cradling. Instinctively she wound her arms around his back, lifting herself closer, pressing her lips to his warm throat, wanting to feel and taste all of him. His mouth grazed across her temples.

'Judy ... I didn't know ... have I hurt you?' Strained bursts of words, interspersed with anxious little kisses, his heart pounding above hers.

'No ... oh no ... it's wonderful,' she breathed, running her hands over the taut muscles of his shoulders, thrusting her fingers through his hair, lifting his head and tilting her own so that their mouths could meet and heighten the sharing of this new inner world of love.

It was a long, long kiss of exploration and discovery, seeking and exulting in every tingling nuance of sensuality, giving and taking with the uninhibited pleasure of total surrender to each other's needs and desires. Then slowly, exquisitely, came the movement inside her, building a liquid warmth which seeped through her body, prickling every nerve-end to vibrant awareness. A quivering tension demanded a more urgent rhythm and her body found an erotic movement of its own. Waves of pleasure gathered force, no longer rippling outwards, but concentrated fiercely on that pulsing inner world which strained to burst into chaotic life.

'Breathe, Judy. Let it happen.'

The breath she had held released itself in ragged gasps and the chaos she had blindly feared was not chaos at all, but an ecstatic spread of beautiful, incredible peace, so warm, so deliciously sweet, so gloriously complete that her whole body moaned in gratitude. And Mal enfolded her in his arms, nursing her contentment with his body, softly now, a slow rhythm of remembrance which kept the new life pulsing with pleasure.

Gently, carefully he moved on to his side, shifting his weight from her yet retaining their exquisite intimacy. He kissed her breasts, caressed her sensitised nakedness, every touch a blissful brush of love. Judy floated on a tide of sensuality, rising to crests of excitement at the erotic play of hands and lips and tongue. She reached for him, returning his lovemaking with intuitive sureness, pleasuring him with a newly learnt freedom, exulting as he trembled under her touch.

She felt the stirring of his need, gasped with delight as his possession hardened into urgency, and moved as one with him to meet his demand. There was no sure control this time, and no longer dazed by her own response, Judy thrilled to his tension, appreciating, gloating over the knowledge of what he was feeling, and climbing with him all the way to that glorious peak of fulfilment once more until it was she holding his shuddering body in her arms, and loving him, loving him with a fierce tenderness which seared her soul.

The long, warm silence of total fulfilment was broken only by the whisper of their breathing and the magical harmony of two hearts beating as one. It was time out of time, too nebulous for words but intensely real with emotion.

'I must be crushing you,' Mal finally whispered, kissing the corners of her mouth with a soft reverence.

'I don't want you to leave me,' she murmured huskily.

'No chance, my darling,' he smiled and pulled her with him as he rolled to one side. He sighed and gently brushed the tumbled curls away from her face. 'You make me feel . . . like I've never felt before. I don't think I could ever have enough of you, Judy Campbell.'

He kissed her forehead, her eyelids, her nose, her mouth, sweet, lingering kisses which moved Judy to tears.

'I knew that first day that you were special, Judy,' he continued softly. 'I didn't know how very special you were but I've never wanted a woman so much.'

'I felt the same way,' she confessed. 'But it was scary, Mal. Too strong, too fast. I didn't know how to handle it.'

He gave a deep chuckle. 'So you threw that herpes nonsense at me and ended up running away.'

She sighed, recalling all the needless heartache of the last nine days. 'Well, jumping into bed on the first day of meeting is not my kind of thing.'

'No. Quite obviously not.' Again came that deep chuckle, a rumble of amusement and delight. 'That's definitely reserved for the second day of meeting.'

It was a shock to realise that was all it was. The second day. She looked at him with startled wonder. The twinkling, teasing green eyes brought a rueful smile to her lips. 'I guess I'm a wanton woman after all.'

'Only for me, my darling.' The twinkle in his eyes changed to a deep, warm glow. 'And you have no idea how very, very possessive that makes me feel.' He reached up and cupped her cheek. 'You belong to me, Judy. And not only in a physical sense. In every sense. You're my woman. I want you here in my house, sharing my life, living with me day and night.'

'Oh, yes,' she breathed, eyes shining with the ultimate happiness of hearing him say what she most wanted to hear. 'Oh, Mal, I do so love you.'

She flung her arms around his neck and kissed him with passionate fervour, and the fervour was returned in equal measure.

'This calls for more champagne, my wanton wench.'

She laughed up at him, intoxicated with love. 'I don't need champagne. I only need you.'

He cocked a mocking eyebrow at her. 'I hate to disappoint you but a man is only capable of so much without some rest and recreation. Besides, I have a fancy to see you ensconced in my kitchen. You can make the salad while I grill some steaks.' He rolled off the bed and tossed her clothes at her. 'And you'd better get dressed. Distractions can be dangerous in a kitchen.'

She lay there grinning at him as he pulled on his jeans. He had a beautiful body and he was all hers. 'To have and to hold from this day forth' ... almost. She wondered how soon they could get married and imagined her mother's delight at the news.

'Come on, you wicked temptress. Want me to dress you?' Mal grinned back at her.

Before she could move he had dived back on to the bed and with much playful wrestling and laughter, he forced her limbs into panties and blouse.

'You forgot my bra,' she teased.

'Abominable garment. I hereby ban bras from

this house. You will, at all times, leave these delicious breasts unfettered.' He pulled the soft lawn tautly over her nipples and kissed them through the material.

Judy sucked in her breath at the sheer eroticism of his love-play. He lifted his head and smiled his satisfaction at the drugged haze in the blue eyes.

'Something tells me we're going to spend a hell of a lot of time in bed, my lovely. We'd better go and eat while I still have enough strength of mind to know what's sensible.' He wrapped her skirt around her and did up the waist-button. 'You can leave the rest undone,' he suggested wickedly.

And she did. It gave her a delicious sense of depravity to leave herself accessible to Mal's touch while doing such a domestic job as cutting up a salad. A feverish excitement coursed through her veins every time his glance lingered on the thrust of her breasts, clearly visible under the thin, white lawn. The few steps between refrigerator and island-bench swung her un-buttoned skirt enough to reveal the soft nakedness of her thighs. She was aware of herself, sexually, sensually aware in a way she had never felt before. And Mal was eating her up with his expressive green eyes.

He turned the steaks and moved up behind her, cupping her breasts with teasing hands as he nuzzled the silky curls away from her neck. 'I'm working up an insatiable appetite. Move in with me tomorrow, Judy. I can't do without you another day.'

His hands slipped down over her stomach, parting her skirt, making her warm flesh shiver as he slid his thumbs under the elastic of her bikini pants. She leaned back, relishing the hard, masculine strength of him.

'I want you, too,' she breathed dreamily. 'But we'll have plenty of time together, Mal. My parents would be shocked if I actually lived with you before we were married.'

His hands stopped their tantalising traverse. His mouth lifted from the curve of throat and shoulder. 'Married? Who said anything about marriage?'

Judy's heart stopped dead. A horrible worm of doubt hollowed out her stomach. Mal's hands moved abruptly, gripping her hips and whirling her around to face him. A heavy frown drew his eyebrows together and there was no desire, no laughter, no teasing in the troubled depths of the green eyes.

'Judy, I'm sorry if you got the wrong idea but I'm not into marriage. No way.'

She stared back at him in pained disbelief. 'I thought you loved me.'

'I do. I adore you. You're the best thing that ever happened to me.'

'And you want me to . . . to shack up with you? Like a . . . a temporary *de facto* wife?'

His grimace held irritation at her in-comprehension. 'No, dammit! Like a woman who wants to be with me because we make a fantastic combination.'

She backed away from him, shaking her head. 'No . . . no . . .'

He reached out for her but she was already beyond easy grasp. He gestured an impatient appeal. 'What do you mean, no?'

'No, I won't.'

Her chest was tight with the pain billowing

inside her. Her legs were heavy, sluggish. It took a concentrated effort to keep them moving. Her mind strained to cope with the agony of separation. All the happiness was draining away. Joy had fled, beaten out by a swift stab of desolation, and the sweet, physical languor which had held her in thrall became a dull, empty ache.

'But you said yes.' Puzzlement and frustation chased across Mal's face.

The island-bench was between them now. Judy picked up her folder, clutching it to her as something solid and familiar to hang on to in a world which had so abruptly shattered into uncertainties. Tears filmed her eyes, an end wash of the despair sweeping through her. 'I thought you loved me,' she repeated, giving him the only truth which explained everything.

'Judy, you're not making sense. Put that folder down, for God's sake!'

She shook her head and hugged the folder to her chest. 'I know where I am with this folder. It's my work. It'll always be part of me. You won't, Mal. That's what you mean, isn't it? No commitment. You just want me to live with you while I satisfy your needs.'

'And yours,' he exploded vehemently, clearly affronted by her attitude. 'It's a two-way street. And as for your work, I'm in a position to steer contracts your way, Judy. Big, commercial work which will spotlight your creativity. We can be a team all the way. Can't you see that?'

The temptation curled around her heart, squeezing it unmercifully. It took every bit of Judy's will-power to thrust it away. Her speech came out stilted and jerky from the effort. 'Yes. Yes, I can. But you don't see it all the way, Mal.

You only see it now. And you expect it to end. Maybe not for a year or two, but when the time comes that you don't want me, or you find someone else who entrances you more, you want to be able to wave me off without a hassle. A civilised parting of the ways.'

'It's left open for you too, Judy. You're free to go as you wish. I don't believe in hog-tying people to you,' he said, full of sweet reason.

Reason. Emotion did not enter into it. Judy ruthlessly killed her own emotion and spoke with cold, cold reason. 'Then I'll go now, Mal. You'd better do something about those steaks. They're burning.'

With angry curse he turned back to the stove and Judy walked out of the kitchen. He caught up with her in the bedroom where she was putting on her joggers. He filled the doorway, blocking her escape route. Judy ignored him, buttoning her skirt, finding her bra and slipping it inside her folder. Her mind orchestrated her movements with steady purpose, stubbornly alive within a body which felt dead.

'You can't mean that, Judy,' came the forceful assertion. 'Not after what we've shared here tonight. You can't just throw that aside.'

She faced him with calm, empty eyes. 'No, I can't. And I wouldn't want to. You gave me a beautiful experience and it'll live with me forever. I'm very grateful for your ... your consideration and ... and everything. You're a wonderful lover, Mal, but I don't want a lover. I wouldn't be happy in that kind of arrangement. It's as simple as that. Please move aside and let me go. I'll be in touch with you about the landscaping.'

'To hell with that! How do you know you

won't be happy? You haven't even tried it. You can't say you haven't been happy with me tonight.'

She dragged in a deep breath to counter the stabbing truth of his words. 'How many times have you tried it, Mal? How many women have . . . lived with you?' she asked dully.

He frowned and made a slicing motion with his hand. 'That's irrelevant to us.'

'Is it? Do you think I'll be the last in the line?'

'How can I know that?' he demanded angrily. 'I can't read the future.'

He didn't want to make a future with her. That's what it added up to, Judy concluded with bitter clarity. An old wound opened and shot forth its pain. 'I'm not good enough for you to marry. That's it, isn't it?'

'Oh, Christ! Not that again!' He half-turned away in disgust then swung back with both hands outflung in frustration. 'Will you get that stupid idea out of your head once and for all? I love you. I want you here, living with me . . .'

'But you won't give me your name.'

His hands clenched and shook. 'What's wrong with your own goddamned name? Why the hell should I have some leech of a wife latching on to my name for a free ride? I won't marry you. I won't marry anyone. I don't believe in bloody marriage!'

His angry outburst pulsed on the air between them, gathering force in the silence which followed, forming a solid wall which would separate them for all time. There was no way across. It was an unequivocal statement. Mal was not going to take it back and Judy could not accept it.

She realised now how stupid she had been to have thought it could ever be otherwise. Mal had not deceived her over his attitude towards marriage. She had known all along he was not a marrying man. Tonight she had deceived herself, grabbing instinctively at her own dream-fulfilment.

'I see,' she said finally, the words barely a whisper. She forced more volume into her voice. 'Then we'd better keep to business from now on.'

'You said you loved me,' he threw at her in accusation, as if she was betraying him.

She closed her eyes against the pain in his. 'You don't want my kind of love, Mal, and I couldn't cope with yours.' It was true. Every principle her upbringing had instilled in her rebelled against accepting his idea of love, but her heart was breaking.

'No.' The tone was hard, decisive. 'I won't let you do this, Judy.'

Her lashes flew up as he moved. She faced his approach with the hard defiance of desperation. 'You have no claim on me, Mal.'

'No claim on you? You gave yourself to me!' His hands took a possessive hold on her upper arms, fingers digging into the soft flesh. 'You're mine!'

'No, I'm not yours. You don't want to own me. You want us to be free. No ties! We can come and go as we please. Well, I'm going. I'm going home. And you have no right to stop me.'

His eyes burnt into hers, determined on searing away her defences. She glared back, equally determined not to surrender to his terms.

'All right. Go home.' He bit the words out as if they were sour to his taste. 'But don't think this is an end to it, Judy. I don't give up on something I want.'

It was no idle threat. He meant it. Judy did not stop to argue. She forced her shaky legs to walk away from him. Now. While she still had the will-power to resist what he was offering. Whether she could resist a determined siege was a very big question mark. There was a huge, fundamental weakness in her defences. She loved him.

CHAPTER EIGHT

THERE was only one thing to do. Get the landscaping done as fast as possible. The sooner she removed herself from Malcolm Stewart's orbit, the sooner she could settle to an existence without him. Time in his company also had to be limited if she was not to succumb to temptation. There was no point in deceiving herself that giving in to him was unthinkable. It was all too thinkable. She could think of little else.

It was no good lying in bed either. She was not going to sleep. Her body was still too alive to the sensations which had been aroused in another bed. And her stomach was rumbling with hunger. She had had no dinner. She had driven straight home from Mal's place, announced to her parents that she had the contract, then retreated swiftly to her bedroom to avoid inquisitive eyes and comments. Her clock-radio now showed 11.38. The house was silent. Judy flung off the bed-clothes and headed for the kitchen.

Having soothed her stomach with baked beans on toast, Judy fetched her folder, a pad and pen and settled herself at the kitchen table. By four in the morning the table was littered with lists of purchases to be made, nurseries to contact, a comprehensive timetable of work-schedules for the various sub-contractors she would employ. She tidied everything away and went to bed, totally exhausted but satisfied that her planning would result in a very efficient operation.

She spent all next day on the telephone; organising, ordering, lining up the necessary tradesmen, checking and re-checking everything against her lists. Some alterations had to be made, a few time-schedules juggled, but by and large she figured there would be no serious hold-ups to her overall scheme. The preparatory work would begin tomorrow and three weeks, a month at most would see the landscaping finished. Provided the weather remained congenial.

A month. Only twenty work-days. Mal would be occupied with his own work. Surely she could avoid him most of the time, Judy thought as a bolster to her resolve, then berated herself for feeling so utterly miserable about it. Some meetings would be unavoidable, indeed necessary. Business courtesy demanded communication with the customer and one of those communications was necessary right now.

With a mixture of reluctance and fluttery anticipation Judy picked up the telephone for the last call of the day. Her fingers trembled as they dialled and she clenched them into a tight fist of determination as the telephone buzzed a summons. She imagined it ringing on Mal's desk, wondered where he would be coming from to answer it, pictured his lithe, athletic body moving with casual grace. Dressed. Undressed. Stop it, she scolded severely.

'Malcolm Stewart.' His voice in her ear.

Cool, calm, steady, she counselled herself. 'It's Judy Campbell. I've organised work to begin on site at eight o'clock tomorrow morning, Mal. Will you be at home at that hour?'

'Yes. I'll be here. Will you?' Very direct and to the point. A very personal point.

Judy's pulse gave a little leap. 'Of course. Naturally I'll be supervising every step. I'll bring you a work-schedule so you'll know who'll be coming and going on any given day. One thing I need to know is the name of the brick you've used in the house so I can order the same for the garden beds.'

'Cadman sandstock from P.G.H.' he answered matter-of-factly.

'Thank you.' She quickly jotted down the name. 'One other thing. Your maps show the location of underground pipes but don't state how far beneath the surface they are.'

'Sixty-five centimetres.'

'Oh good! No trouble then. That's all, Mal. I'll see you in the morning.'

'Judy . . .'

She was already congratulating herself on having handled the call well, even replacing the receiver when the tense urgency in his voice halted her. Caution demanded she cut him off but she hesitated, longing to hear anything he had to say.

'Yes?' Her voice quavered on the word and she cursed herself for a fool.

She heard his faint expulsion of breath before he spoke. Softly. Persuasively. Invitingly, 'Come and have dinner with me, Judy. Let's talk.'

Oh God! She ached to be with him, of him, belonging as they had last night. He could evoke a total awareness of himself even over the telephone. 'I . . . I've work to do. We can talk in the morning, Mal. 'Bye now.'

She slammed the receiver down before temptation could catch her in its thrall again. In sheer panic she rushed out to the kitchen where her mother was preparing dinner and her father was enjoying his customary pre-dinner sherry.

'Dad, would it be asking too much for you to come in Alf's place tomorrow? Just tomorrow. Please?'

Judy knew immediately that she had blundered. Both parents turned to her in surprise and as if to highlight her unusual burst of anxiety, Judy flushed, a ghastly, self-conscious, burning crimson, which she then felt forced to explain.

'I . . . it's . . . the job's so important to me. I'd feel more . . . more confident that everything will start off smoothly if you're there. That probably sounds silly but . . .' She trailed off, not sure if she was improving the situation or making it more curious by floundering so hopelessly.

'It's not like you to get into a flap, Judy,' her father remarked slowly.

His eyes narrowed and Judy could almost hear the shrewd calculation clickety-clicking in his all-too-knowing mind. She wished he had not seen Malcolm Stewart kissing her. And her kissing him. Fortunately her mother came to the rescue, apparently quite pleased that her daughter was not as aggressively independent as she had suspected.

'I can manage the office tomorrow, Drew, and with Alf around to handle the heavy work for me, there's no reason why you shouldn't go. Billy will be pleased, too. Much as he likes Alf, you know how much he loves working with you. It'll be like a family outing with the three of you. And besides, you should give Judy your support. The Lord knows she's been your right-hand in the nursery.'

'All right, Judy, if that's what you want,' he

agreed in a far too measured tone for Judy's comfort.

It was the strength of the family behind her that she wanted. No . . . needed. The living proof of the alternative to what Malcolm Stewart was offering. 'Thanks, Dad,' she mumbled, then turned quickly to her mother. 'Sure you don't mind being left holding the fort, Mum?'

Her mother smiled. 'It's a good excuse for neglecting the housework. And I want you to sleep tonight,' she added pointedly. 'I realise this job's important to you, Judy, but so's a proper rest. Do be a sensible girl and go to bed early tonight.'

'Yes, Mum,' she said meekly.

Her father gave Judy another searching look but reserved comment, much to her relief. The conversation over dinner revolved around the landscaping job and Judy was able to talk quite naturally about the work-plan she had organised. Afterwards she casually withdrew to her bedroom and did a professional job of typing up the lists she wanted to hand to Mal in the morning. Then she began on a formal presentation of sketches, intent on documenting every detail of her work for future reference. A sharp tap on the door broke her concentration.

'Judy, may I come in?'

'Yes,' she answered automatically, although her heart gave a wary little skip. Her father rarely presented himself in her bedroom. To do so tonight was decidedly ominous. She felt herself growing very defensive as he opened the door.

His gaze swept over her desk before fixing on her wide-eyed look of enquiry. 'It's eleven o'clock. Your mother tells me you were up 'til dawn this morning. Don't you think it'd be wise to go to bed now?'

Judy glanced at the clock in innocent surprise. 'Didn't realise it'd got so late. Thanks, Dad.'

He nodded, seemed about to go, then hesitated, the sharp blue eyes scanning her face, probing for the underlying strain. 'What's wrong, Judy? Anything I can help you with?'

'No,' she replied too quickly, then forced a smile. 'You'll be helping me by coming tomorrow, Dad. That's all I need. A bit of moral support.'

'Moral support,' he repeated with a heavy intonation which was too suggestive for Judy's comfort.

She put down her pencil and made a business of tidying her desk. 'Well, more like insurance that nothing will go wrong. Not that I expect it to, but . . .' She shrugged and stood up. 'Guess I will go to bed now. Good night, Dad.'

'You can always depend on our support, Judy, no matter what you choose to do. I hope you know that,' he said quietly.

'Yes. Yes, I do. Thanks, Dad.'

'Good night, love.'

Love. Family. Tears pricked Judy's eyes as the door closed on her father. This was what Mal rejected, yet it was so important to Judy, what she had always known and had always imagined for herself, a family unit secured by the steadfast commitment of love and loyalty. But she loved Mal, and she believed that he loved her. Perhaps she was wrong to take such an inflexible stand on the issue of marriage.

She had spurned his proposition because it had fallen short of her ideal, but Mal's background could not have engendered a favourable view of marriage. As a child he had been the pawn in a hostile divorce and clearly his personal experiences with women had not encouraged him to find the legal knot attractive. His cynicism was probably as deep-rooted as her idealism.

For the first time in her life Judy groped outside the framework of her own long-held ideas and tried to accept another viewpoint. Living together without benefit of marriage was a common practice these days. It was socially acceptable to the vast majority. Judy had always rationalised such relationships by assuming either there was a good reason why marriage was impracticable, or the couple concerned were merely making use of each other until something better turned up.

She was not one to sit in judgment on how other people chose to live. That was their business. If there was some impediment to a marriage between her and Mal, some concrete reason she could understand, then that would have given rise to a different situation. But as far as she could see, he simply did not want to give himself to a serious commitment, and it was not in Judy's nature to give herself to less. An open-ended relationship seemed to her a desert of emotional quicksand where any step could be the end. Instead of trust, it sowed fear and uncertainty.

Yet she had felt certain of Mal's love last night. Perhaps if she lived with him, eventually he might feel happy enough with her to make it a permanent arrangement. If she did not try his way there would be no chance of that happening, but if she tried and failed to change his attitude ... and she would fail, Judy thought with depressing certainty. If Mal was not prepared to offer marriage now, the offer was even less likely to come when he had what he wanted without tying himself legally to her.

And what of children? She imagined herself saying, 'I want a child', and Mal replying, 'If that's what you want, go ahead, but it's your choice, your responsibility.' No joint commitment. Open-ended meant not being able to take his support for granted. It was a two-way street all right, with a dividing line down the centre and each going his own way except when mutual desire coincided in parking next to each other for a while.

No. It might be right for him. For some other woman who valued her freedom. Not for Judy. She wanted ties. Needed them. Her reaction last night had been instinctive, protecting all that she believed in. The decision to reject his offer had been right for her. No matter how much it hurt she had to turn her back on him or she would never have contentment. Having settled the question once more, Judy went to bed and slept peacefully.

Nevertheless, when morning came and she was on her way to Mal's home—the home she had been invited to share—Judy ruefully concluded that it was one thing to make a pragmatic decision, quite another to keep emotional turmoil under tight discipline. She loved Mal and every kilometre closer to him added a taut measure of anticipation, no matter how scathingly she spoke to herself. The knowledge that her father and brother were in the semi-loader travelling behind her was the only steadying factor which was unshakeable. She did not have to face Mal alone.

She did not know how she was going to face him at all. The memory of their intimacy was hard enough to handle without having it sharpened to immediacy with his presence. Somehow she had to carry off her role as landscaper with polite aplomb, carefully avoiding any trap that Mal might set. It was simply a question of holding out until he gave up on her. Only it was not simple. Not when her nerves were turning her stomach into a queasy pit.

She turned the pick-up truck into the driveway, watched in the rear-vision mirror to check that the semi-loader followed, then signalled her father to park next to her outside the privacy wall. Rather than seek Mal out to announce her arrival Judy had decided to set up work first. Besides, it made for a less personal situation if he was to find her on site in the company of her father and Billy. She had no doubt that Mal would come looking for her.

They were undoing the chains which had anchored the bob-cat to the float when he strode through the gateway, the quickness of expectancy in his gait. He stopped dead the moment he saw who had accompanied Judy. The smile of greeting stiffened and when he resumed his approach the handsome face showed only a polite mask.

'Good morning,' he said pleasantly, looking every inch the successful businessman in his brown business-suit, well and truly a cut above the work-drill favoured by Judy's family.

'Hello, Mal,' Billy said brightly, unaware that anything had changed since this man had been introduced as Judy's friend.

'Morning, Mr Stewart,' Drew Campbell

nodded, his voice carrying a note of cautious formality.

Judy was very conscious of her father's watchful gaze and did her utmost to appear relaxed. 'Good morning, Mal.' To her immense surprise the words came out smoothly and she continued with more confidence. 'We'll be pouring the foundations for the garden beds this afternoon. Dad brought the bob-cat to dig the trenches. We'll also be rotary-hoeing the grounds and moving some earth around, hence the tractor, the blade and the plough. The top-soil and bush-rocks will be delivered this afternoon.'

'I see. Quite a busy day,' Mal commented tightly. The green eyes were strangely opaque, revealing nothing.

'Every day will be busy,' Judy informed him breezily. 'I'm sure you'd like to see the job finished as soon as possible.'

He ignored her last remark and turned to her father. 'I didn't realise you'd be working with Judy, Mr Campbell.'

Judy sensed the belligerence behind the smooth civility and tensed as her father swung around to answer, a half-smile on his lips which did not reach his eyes. The blue gaze was decidedly reserved.

'Judy knows I'll do the best job for her and I'd be a poor father not to give her any support she requires in her first big job.' The words were slow and measured, as if testing out the ground. 'Lovely day, isn't it?'

There was a chilling little pause before Mal answered, 'Quite!' The word was snapped off. He turned to Judy, one eyebrow slanting emphasis to the mockery in his eyes. 'I believe you mentioned bringing me a work-schedule.'

'Oh yes. It's in the truck. Excuse me a moment. I'll get it for you,' she babbled, anxious for this awkward meeting to be at an end. She handed him the manila folder into which she had stapled the typed work-sheets. 'I'll inform you of any changes or delays and I'll have fully documented lay-outs of all the landscaping drawn up for you as soon as possible.'

He flicked through the pages and was frowning heavily by the time he came to the last sheet. 'All this has been organised in one day?' The question carried surprise and irritation.

'Yes, I'm afraid it took a whole day, but now we can forge ahead with the work,' Judy replied blithely, pretending this was nothing but a business discussion.

The green eyes seemed to be simmering with resentment in the short silence which followed her statement. Then his gaze swept around, acknowledging Billy and Drew Campbell again. 'I'll give Judy a set of keys to the house and cabana. Use anything you want while you're here so long as everything is locked up again before you go each day.'

'Very kind of you,' Drew Campbell said affably.

'I want to see you, Judy. Privately.' It was a peremptory summons to accompany him into the house and he set off without giving her a chance to refuse.

'Be right back, Dad,' she muttered and hurried after Mal, hoping that he did not mean to use this opportunity to attack her defences.

He did not wait for her, did not even turn to see if she was following. He stood stiffly at the front door, holding it open until she had passed through, then shutting it with a firmness which barely stopped short of a slam.

'What the hell are you playing at, Judy?' he snapped angrily.

She met the blazing green eyes with all the coolness she could command. 'I'm not playing. I'm here to work.'

'With your whole damned family in tow! You think I can't read the scenario? I suppose if you're not out of here in five minutes your father'll be knocking on the door with a shotgun in his hands.'

The impassioned speech was laced with such bitterness that Judy was appalled. It took a moment for his implication to sink in and then it struck her forcefully, driving tears to her eyes and completely shattering her careful composure. She struggled to retain some dignity, speaking unsteadily but with undiminished pride. 'My family is here to help me fulfil my contract with you. That is our only interest. We work together in everything. That's what families are all about, Mal. Loyalty and love.'

His jaw tightened as if he was clenching his teeth. Without another word he turned on his heel and headed for the stairs. Judy did not follow this time. He had hurt her enough. She would not go running after him. She simply stood there, regathering her strength before going out to join her father.

'Come on. The keys are in my study,' Mal flung at her as he clattered down the stairs.

To hell with his keys! I'll do without them, Judy decided impulsively, then thought better of it. There was not only her family to consider. Other workmen would require the conveniences of the cabana and it would be stupid of her to deny herself the use of a telephone on site. She swallowed her pride and walked at a sedate pace, in no hurry to face his anger and contempt again. Both were totally undeserved and she fiercely resented his assumption.

She reached the doorway of the study and halted there, watching him rummage impatiently through a desk-drawer. He tossed the keys on the desk, apparently unprepared to cross the room and hand them to her. Again Judy was tempted to scorn the use of them, but determined to act in a professional manner, she held her head high and took the necessary paces to gain possession of them.

'Thank you. I'll personally see that everything is securely locked at the end of each day,' she said coldly. She was at the study door again when his voice whipped after her.

'Damn you, Judy! You know I didn't force myself on you. It was what we both wanted.'

She drew a deep breath and consciously squared her shoulders before looking back. 'I don't know why you're so angry, Mal. I haven't suggested otherwise,' she said flatly.

'Then why walk out on me?'

'I told you why.'

'Holding yourself to ransom,' he jeered, his face twisting with violent emotion. 'You're cheating both of us, Judy.'

The bitter accusation was too much for Judy to swallow. She swung around to face him, chin lifted proudly, eyes stabbing him with scorn. 'There is no price on love, Malcolm Stewart. What I feel ... felt ... for you cannot be bought.'

'Oh no?' he sneered. 'You said you loved me but you're intent on withholding any expression of that love unless I sign a marriage contract which effectively gives half my property to you. Quite a bride-price, wouldn't you say?'

The blood drained from her face. For one awful moment Judy thought she was going to faint, so sickened was she by his reasoning. Her hand automatically sought support, finding the door-jamb and gripping the architrave as she swayed.

'I did say I loved you. I gave you all I had to give thinking ... believing ... that you felt as I did. I offered you a whole lifetime of loving. But you don't want it.' The pain of loss sharpened her voice. 'I would be cheating myself if I lived with a man who valued my love less than his personal freedom and property. Even if you offered me marriage now, I wouldn't accept. Either a commitment is freely given or it's not worth the paper it's written on. Keep your freedom, Mal. Keep your property. I'll keep myself for a man who loves me as I love him. A man who sees marriage as a gain, not a loss.'

'How can you speak of keeping yourself for someone else? You've given yourself to me. You're mine!' he insisted vehemently.

Tears of desolation filmed her eyes. 'No. I'm not yours. You had first claim, that's all. You didn't think enough of me to take up ownership. You have no property rights on me. No contract was signed,' she said bitterly. 'There's no more to be said. Please excuse me. As far as I'm concerned the matter is closed.'

Tears were gathering behind her eyes. She had to go before she broke down completely and lost her dignity before a man who granted her none. She about-turned and marched across the living room.

'Oh, it's a great love you have when you can shut it off like that!' he jeered.

He knees wobbled. Shut it off! My God! If only she could. She reached out for the bannister and clutched it in relief, needing it to haul her safely up the stairs. Something crashed to the floor in the study. Mal strode after her roaring with frustration.

'God damn you! How can you turn your back on what we shared the other night? Marriage is an outdated tradition which stinks of corruption, and I won't be caught up in it. We had something good and pure and unsullied by greed. Why can't it stay that way?'

She neither paused nor looked back. She watched her feet moving steadily upwards and away from him. 'If you found it so good, why don't you want to hold on to it forever?' she countered flatly.

'Why do you think I asked you to live with me?' he shouted after her.

She turned at the top step and surveyed him with all the bleak clarity of total disillusionment. Aggression emanated from him, the green eyes glowering in mutinous challenge, chin thrust out in stubborn defiance, legs stiffly apart . . . a man who was used to getting his own way and was reacting badly to being refused.

'I'm going out to work. I'll do my best to enhance your house with a landscape which will add value to your property. I'm sure that'll give you more lasting satisfaction than anything else I could give you. When I hand you back these keys, Mal, it'll be finished, and I never want to see you again.'

The tanned skin of his face flushed a dark red. 'So be it then. I won't crawl after you.'

Her heart twisted into a tortured knot. She nodded and took her leave of him, knowing the parting was final and irrevocable. Once outside, pride gave Judy the strength to throw herself into work with an intensity of purpose which drew several dry observations from her father. She ignored them at first but finally spelled out an answer which silenced him.

'I will not rest until this job is completed and it's going to be the best damned job that any landscaper has ever done. I will not compromise on any detail and I'll give Malcolm Stewart his money's worth down to the very last cent. So don't hassle me, Dad. I have to do this my way.'

She went about it like a woman obsessed, not allowing anything else to exist for her. Work was an anaesthetic to the pain she refused to even recognise. Everything had to be done to the highest standard; not one ripple in the lawn which was laid, not one bush-rock whose shape or placement displeased her eye, not one tree or shrub which was not a beautiful specimen.

Each night she poured hours into the most meticulous documentation. Everything planted was numbered on her sketches and each number had a typed sheet of its own, giving the formal and popular name of each specimen, a full description of its notable characteristics, the name of the nursery from which it had been purchased and the date of purchase. Most nights she fell into bed in a state of exhaustion but she had only to wake in the morning and she was on

the go again, nervous energy driving her through
the day.

She saw little of Mal and did not speak to him
at all. There was no change in her planned
schedule. The weather smiled on her. The
occasional shower of rain fell in the evening,
helping her work, not hindering it. Judy's
satisfaction grew with each completed area. By
the end of the second week she could stand on the
back patio and look with pride on what she had
envisaged and accomplished. The landscape was
impressive now and it showed the promise of
becoming spectacular in years to come.

By Wednesday afternoon of the third week
there was little left for her to do. All the major
planting had been done. The front lawn was
being laid. The next two days would see the
concrete kerb of the driveway being poured. She
took the punnets of vegetable seedlings and herbs
down to the kitchen garden and began setting
them out in the prepared beds. Tomatoes,
lettuce, parsley, mint, chives, thyme, spinach . . .
her mouth twisted into a wry grimace as she
planted those seedlings in the wet soil. She had
been so innocently happy when spinach had been
discussed.

The gate to the front courtyard opened. Judy
glanced up expecting to see Billy and was totally
discomfited to find Malcolm Stewart standing
there. Not once had he sought her out since that
ugly confrontation the first morning. Judy had
sometimes seen the Aston Martin leaving in the
morning but she had always been gone before it
returned in the evening.

He just stood there gazing at her with those
provocative green eyes and a rush of resentment

brought hot colour to her cheeks. What did he want? Why didn't he speak? The silence grated on her nerves.

'I'm planting your spinach,' she said defensively.

'So I see. You look exhausted.'

She bridled at his tone of concern. 'It's been a tiring day,' she muttered.

'They must have all been tiring days for so much to have been accomplished in so short a time. It all looks magnificent, Judy.'

Her cheeks burnt even more hotly. She did not want his praise. She did not want to accept anything from him.

'Thank you,' she mumbled, fiercely wishing he would go away and leave her alone. She had managed to block him out of her mind most of the time. It was better if he did not rouse her out of the peaceful, zombie-like state she had nurtured.

'You haven't asked me for any more money,' he said rather tentatively.

She glanced up warily. 'Is there a financial problem? You said not to cut costs.'

'No problem. I didn't want you worrying over meeting bills, that's all.'

'The nursery can meet them. I'll post you a full account of everything once the job is completed.'

He nodded. Judy concentrated on transferring spinach seedlings from punnet to garden bed, intent on removing herself from his disturbing presence as soon as possible. He was showing no inclination to move.

'When do you expect to finish?'

'Monday. If the fine weather holds.' She

clicked the empty punnet into the others and wiped the dirt from her hands.

'Well, you certainly have created a showcase for your remarkable talent, Judy. I had some business associates here over the weekend. They were most impressed,' he said with what seemed unnecessary emphasis.

Judy brushed herself down and gathered up the punnets. 'That must have pleased you. If you'll excuse me, I'll be going home now.'

His mouth thinned in exasperation at the blank façade she offered him. 'Doesn't it please you?' he demanded tightly.

'Yes. But I'm satisfied no matter what anyone else thinks.'

'Quite the self-contained person, aren't you?' he snapped, then made an obvious effort to recover his equanimity. 'Judy, I have a proposition which should interest you,' he said with quiet deliberation.

Instantly her eyes flared with hostile life. 'I thought I made it clear that I'm not interested in any proposition you have to offer.'

'Will you just listen to me for a few minutes? It's not what you think,' he cut back swiftly.

Green eyes met blue in a war of wills and into that tense moment fell a familiar voice.

'Malcolm? Where are you? I can hear you talking out here somewhere.' The gate was pushed open and Vivien Holgate stood there, groomed in the expensive elegance which spelled out a very special social engagement.

'I didn't expect you quite so early, Viv,' Mal said with a touch of irritation.

'Oh, I thought I'd give myself time to look over all this marvellous landscaping you've been raving on about.' She bestowed a gracious smile on Judy. 'Aren't you the clever girl? It was very naughty of you to describe yourself as a mere turf-deliverer. And speaking of turf, I couldn't get that stupid half-wit out the front to move the truck in the driveway, so I had to park on the roadside and walk up.'

'Viv . . .' Mal began in a tone of reproof, throwing an anxious look at Judy.

He was given no time to smooth over his lady-friend's tactless gaffe. Judy lashed out with the ferocity of a lioness whose cub had been mauled. 'That half-wit is my brother. His mental age might be that of an eight-year-old but he is not stupid. If you'd taken the trouble to listen to him he would've explained that he's not allowed to drive the truck. I'm sorry you were inconvenienced. The blame is mine. Not Billy's. I'll see that the truck is removed immediately. Good afternoon to both of you.'

'Oh dear!' The marble-smooth forehead creased into lines. 'I didn't mean . . .'

'Judy . . .'

She knocked Mal's outstretched arm aside, ignored Vivien's attempt at apology, stalked through the courtyard and broke into a run down the driveway, waving a summons to Billy who was still unrolling turf.

'Get in the truck. We're going home.'

'But I haven't finished.'

'Doesn't matter. Leave it. We're going now.'

Billy obeyed without further question, responding automatically to the urgent demand in his sister's voice. There was a shout behind her as Judy climbed into the cabin but a mountain of inner rage made a reply as dangerous as a volcano exploding. The ignition key was given a vicious twist. Her foot stabbed the accelerator. In a matter of seconds the truck was hurtling down the driveway.

Judy bared her teeth at the silver Mercedes on the roadside, hating the polished sleekness which so symbolised its owner. Vivien Holgate. The bared teeth gnashed over the name. The supercilious, superior bitch! She was a good match for Malcolm Stewart, Judy thought furiously. Devious, designing, dazzling with sophistication! And just how sophisticated could a man get, propositioning one woman with another all lined up for a night out ... and a night in, no doubt.

So much for his hotly declared love for Judy Campbell! It had cooled fast enough, fanned by the frustration of having his cosy little plans rejected. She had done herself the biggest favour of her life walking out on that ... that amoral bastard! And marriage? Huh! What a laugh! No respecter of marriage was he, indulging in adultery with his friend's wife. Easy come, easy go. Musical beds. And Judy Campbell was no exception. She had been a pushover to his charm. Thank God she hadn't stayed pushed over. It was plain to see she was instantly replaceable.

And to think she had fancied his feeling for her had been genuine! Sheer self-deception! Blind stupidity! He was not worth another thought. She would rip him out of her heart and mind and never, never, never give him memory-space again.

'Why are you crying, Judy?'

Billy's innocent question startled her. She had not realised that tears were trickling down her cheeks. She dashed them away but there seemed to be an exhaustable well of tears which could not be stemmed.

'I've got sore eyes. Soon be home,' she assured her brother, knowing he would become distressed if she admitted to being upset.

Damn Malcolm Stewart to hell! I won't cry over him. I won't! Judy seethed, her vision becoming more blurred by the minute. When she finally reached home she made a dash for her bedroom, locked the door, and cried her heart out.

CHAPTER NINE

'WOULD you come back to the house with me for a few minutes, Judy? I have something to show you.'

It was a demand, smoothly coated in politeness but a demand nevertheless, and the sting of it was that Judy had no excuse for refusing to go with him. She and Alf were having their morning-tea break with the men who had been working on the kerb. They were sitting in a relaxed group near one of the brick pillars. Her presence was not required on the site and she would not win any respect from the men by snubbing Malcolm Stewart. He was a big man in their eyes, an important personage, a somebody, and they were pleased to find themselves working on his property.

She had seen Mal's approach and studiously ignored it, just as she had disassociated herself from his perfunctory little chat with the men. He had stood next to her and she had continued sipping her tea as if he was not there at all. Now he was forcing her to acknowledge him and short of being impossibly rude, she had no choice but to go along with him. She put her mug down, stood up and glanced pointedly at her watch before meeting his eyes with a steely blue gaze.

'I hope this won't take long, Mal. I'm a labourer short and I haven't time to waste.'

'It won't be wasted.' He waved her to walk beside him. He was holding the front door open for her when he asked, 'Where's Billy today?'

Judy flashed him a scathing look as she stepped past him. 'At the nursery where he won't be the target of disparaging remarks from your friends.'

'You're over-reacting, Judy. Viv didn't mean to give offence. It was a thoughtless remark, that's all. She asked me to pass on an apology.'

Judy gritted her teeth and swallowed back a wave of belligerence. She wouldn't waste her breath on Vivien Holgate. Mal closed the door and looked at her expectantly. No way was Judy going to meekly accept a second-hand apology from that woman.

'You said you have something to show me,' she reminded him tersely.

His breath whistled out in a short sigh. 'In the study,' he said, making a wry little grimace.

They walked down the hallway together, yet very much apart as far as Judy was concerned. She tensed as they approached the study, reluctant to enter the room which had twice been the scene of painful turmoil. Mal stood back and gestured for her to enter first. She took quick steps, anxious that this scene be met and dealt with promptly.

The diorama of the Fairway Tourist Centre sat on the desk, surrounded by detailed architectural sketches of the finished façade. Judy stopped well short of it, determined to have no interest in Malcolm Stewart's work or anything about him.

'As I said yesterday, I have a proposition for you. How would you like to do all the landscaping for the Fairway Tourist Centre?'

The sharp tension of imminent battle suddenly drained into a bottomless pit of despair. Judy's whole body wanted to sag but pride kept it rigid. He was offering her a job in a million, a job no landscaper in the entire country would turn down. She had thought the landscaping of Malcolm Stewart's property would spark off her career but its importance paled into insignificance compared to what was being offered to her now.

Yet she could not take it. It was from him. She had not earned this chance. She had not done enough to deserve it. Only his influence could have swung it her way and he certainly wouldn't have championed her cause out of the goodness of his heart. There would be a price to pay on his patronage.

'Wouldn't you like to see what the job entails?' he asked invitingly.

He had moved around behind the desk. Judy had not moved at all. Nor did she now, except to lift the heavy veil of her lashes. There was a stillness about Mal which suggested tension. Even the green eyes were still, intensely concentrated upon her, watching, waiting for her reaction.

Her mouth was dry. Her throat was dry. She felt dry and withered up all through. 'No.' The word came out like a croak of doom.

He frowned. His hands lifted and swept over the diorama, urging her to consider what was laid out for her. 'Think what it could mean to you, Judy,' he said insistently.

She swallowed a couple of times, moistening her mouth because she now knew what to answer him. 'I'm not prepared to pay the price.'

An angry flush crept up his neck. 'There is no price. The job is yours if you want it.'

She eyed him sceptically. 'You must have done a hard bit of arguing to get it for me, Mal. I'm not so blind with ego and ambition that I can't see behind the lines.'

'Yes. I had to do some convincing,' he admitted shortly, 'but your work here was the clinching argument.'

She shook her head. 'Without your support I wouldn't have even been in the running.'

'So what's wrong with my support? A job like this is always swung one way or another by someone's support.'

She suddenly realised it was futile arguing the point. 'The answer's no.'

His mouth thinned into grim lines and the green eyes glittered dangerously. 'Would you mind telling me why? I've gone to a lot of trouble to give you this chance.'

Her chin came up in proud defiance. 'I will not accept anything from you, Malcolm Stewart. I don't want to work with you, see you, or be associated with you in any shape or form.'

The glitter faded from his eyes, leaving them dull and bleak. 'I see.' The words were so soft they were barely audible. He sighed and continued in a gentle tone which was more telling than sharpness. 'From your point of view it's easier to hate me, isn't it? Yet I'm the same person you loved. I haven't changed. I simply refused to go through with a ceremony which I see as a hypocritical farce.'

Bitterness poured out of the wounds he had opened. 'Of course you see it as a hypocritical farce! Go back to Vivien Holgate and destroy another marriage!'

Having thrown down the unanswerable exit-line, Judy tossed her head in haughty disdain, turned on her heel and swiftly and determinedly put him behind her. Three more working days and he would be permanently behind her. And the days could not go fast enough for her.

His job offer had only been a bribe to get her into his bed, Judy fumed as she tramped up the stairs. If people admired her landscaping here, then the jobs would come. She did not need Malcolm Stewart's dubious patronage. And no way would she accept it! No way!

The clack of footsteps on the tiled hallway warned her that she was being followed. Pride and anger dictated that she not look back. Her hand was reaching for the brass door-knob when she was roughly hauled backwards and flattened against a wall.

'And don't you move until I've had my say!' Mal bit out threateningly.

She glared back at him, wildly tempted to spit in his face, but the face which looked thunderously down at her was in no mood to brook defiance. She compressed her lips and waited, her ears stubbornly closed to anything he had to say.

He read her non-receptivity with mounting exasperation. 'Goddammit! You're an impossible bloody woman! Vivien Holgate's never meant a goddammed thing to me!' His fist punched the air then shook menacingly at her. 'Do you think I was with her last night?' he shouted, then clipped each word out with grated fury. 'She came to take me to a meeting. Which I went to. With her husband. He drove me home. She went to a bloody fashion parade!'

He paused to suck in a calming breath then continued in a more controlled manner, his eyes stabbing her with all the righteousness of a man falsely judged. 'I've done everything I can for you . . .'

Judy could not hold herself in. 'Not for me,' she retorted fiercely. 'For you! You've done everything you can to get your own selfish way. You weren't thinking of what I want. Or need.'

He drew back as if she had struck him. The face which had been contorted with emotion stiffened into hard, proud lines. When he spoke his voice chilled the heat from her blind fury.

'I thought I did know what you wanted. And needed. It seems I was wrong. But I'm not the only one, Judy. You're not only wrong, you're terribly and totally wrong. If you have any objectivity and self-honesty you'll eventually concede that. I'll give you the weekend to consider the Fairway job. Maybe by Monday you can talk to me without prejudice.'

This time it was he who turned on his heel and marched away, stiff-legged, shoulders straight, his whole bearing one of uncompromising dignity. He did not once glance back to see what effect his ultimatum had had on her. He had delivered it. That was it. Finis. Wipe-out. Until Monday.

Judy was more shaken than she cared to admit. She had to push herself away from the wall and force her legs to walk to the front door. Once outside, pure instinct carried her to the truck. She would not let herself think. There were too many disturbing ideas floating around in her head and if she let them take hold, the strong wall of principles she had built around herself might become less solid. She stared at the rolls of turf still to be unloaded. Here was work to do. Lots and lots of mindless work. She heaved a roll down and headed for the bare section which still had to be grassed.

'Thought I was to do the carrying,' Alf remarked as he met her on his way back to the truck for more.

'No point in wasting a walk,' Judy muttered in reply.

'Well, you've got plenty to lay over there,' he pointed out.

He spoke the truth. She had been with Malcolm Stewart longer than a few minutes. A whole lifetime longer, it seemed. She set about unrolling the turf, fitting it together with meticulous care. The powerful thrum of the Aston Martin's engine gave notice of Mal's departure. Judy did not glance around. Her ears automatically registered the sound until it was swallowed into distant noises. She waited for relief to soothe her troubled soul but relief did not come. The worms of guilt and self-doubt which Mal had set slithering around her mind suddenly developed suckers and demanded attention.

She had been wrong about Vivien. Badly wrong. Jealousy had leapt to assumptions which had been unwarranted. Jealousy and envy. There had been no real evidence for her suspicions; an admiring comment from Mal, Vivien's own assurance in her charms and her utter sophistication which had dimmed Judy's sense of self-worth.

Twice Mal had denied any interest in Vivien Holgate and Judy had to admit it would be unreasonable prejudice not to believe him now. There was ample evidence of his single-minded interest in herself. He had pursued her beyond two rejections, both of them hurtful and insulting. She had used attack as defence, lashing out at him because she feared her own weakness.

Mal had put his finger on the truth back there in the study. It was easier for her to hate him, easier to brand him an amoral, uncaring man who did not deserve her love. It gave her decision more justification. Not that it needed justification, Judy insisted to herself. So she had been wrong about Vivien. And wrong about the shallowness of Mal's love. She had still been right about not living with him. So nothing had changed. And she stubbornly clung to that thought all day.

However, it was not so easy to dismiss him from her mind as she lay awake in the darkness of night. Mal's taunt about self-honesty forced a re-appraisal of their relationship. She could no longer doubt that he loved her. Everything he had done was consistent with loving her. He had not used the landscaping of his property to persuade her into his bed. The contract had been given, free and clear. He had even controlled his own desire to make her initiation into lovemaking as beautiful and pleasurable as possible. He had offered Judy everything but marriage.

And despite all that had been said between them, he still cared. Very deeply. It could not have been easy to swing the Fairway landscaping her way. And that, too, he had insisted was free and clear. No strings attached. The strings were coiled in her own heart, aching to be released so they could spring back to him, binding her to a love which she still saw as doomed.

But was it doomed? Maybe a live-in relationship could work. Maybe he would give her the emotional security she had imagined only existed within marriage. She had not trusted enough in his love to believe that possible but maybe she was wrong. Terribly and totally wrong. One way or another she had to make up her mind by Monday.

Judy did not see Mal on Friday which was both a relief and an aching disappointment. It did not rain. The kerb of the driveway was completed on time. The cement would be dried out enough for the gravel to be spread on Monday. The lawn had to be brought to the very edge of the kerb, a mere tidying up process which would only take a couple of hours. Even if it rained on Monday it could be done.

The weekend was the longest, most miserable two days Judy had ever endured. She could not work, eat or sleep. She tried to concentrate on the paperwork necessary to give a complete account of expenses but her mind could not get the essential figures into coherent order. She made a mess of everything.

Sunday night came and her nerves were wound so tightly that she was ready to snap at anyone who even looked sideways at her. The wary disapproval of her parents and Billy's reproachful glances made her feel guilty but she could not help herself. Sleep finally came in the early hours of Monday morning and it was the sleep of utter exhaustion.

When her eyelids lifted again it was almost noon. Despite feeling groggy Judy flew out of bed and dressed in a state of near panic. The last day! And she had almost slept through it! She raced out to the kitchen and accosted her mother. 'Why didn't you wake me?'

'You needed the sleep. No job is worth a

nervous breakdown, Judy. Besides, you have nothing to worry about. Your father's there and he'll see that the driveway is finished properly.'

'But the turf near the kerb still has to be laid,' she protested.

Her mother heaved a sigh of exasperation. 'It won't be the end of the world if it has to be left until tomorrow, but it's only lunch-time. Billy's cut and rolled the turf. You can go after you've had something to eat. Not before. You've worked yourself into a state of collapse and I will not stand for it, Judy, career or no career. Now you sit yourself at this table and calm down.'

Judy tamely obeyed the sit-down command. It had been many years since her mother had used that tone of authority. It brooked no opposition. Judy knew from old that arguing was pointless. When Tess Campbell took a stand she was immovable. An omelette and salad was pushed on her and Judy forced them down while her mother kept up a steady grumble about overwork, letting Judy know that she did not approve of her daughter's manner or behaviour.

'Sorry, Mum. Didn't mean to be like a bear with a sore head,' Judy apologised as she rose from the table. She gave her mother a hug and a quick peck on the cheek. 'Thanks for lunch. 'Bye now.'

'Must you go?'

Judy was already at the kitchen door when the anxious question stopped her. She looked back to find her mother's eyes sharp with worry. Before Judy could answer, her mother plunged on.

'Oh, never mind.' She shook her head wearily. 'Just take it easy, dear. Remember there's always tomorrow.'

'Yes, Mum. 'Bye.'

But there wasn't tomorrow, Judy thought despondently as she drove towards Mal's place. This afternoon she had to give him an answer and there were only a few short hours left in which to make her decision.

Her father was working the blade over the last of the gravel heaps when Judy arrived. She parked the truck on the roadside and could not help feeling a swell of pride as she surveyed the elegant sweep of the driveway. The cement kerb had whitened with drying out and the artistically curved line certainly gave the symmetrical emphasis for which she had aimed. The red-brown gravel not only complemented the brickwork of the privacy wall but provided an attractive contrast to the green of the lawn. Yes, it was right. Beautifully right. She could not have planned better.

Her father grinned at her and gave a cheery wave. She waved back and then wandered around the newly planted trees and shrubs, checking that all were doing well. When the gravel had been distributed evenly everywhere, Drew Campbell drove the tractor on to the semi-loader and Judy hurried down to help him chain it on.

'Great job, Dad. Thanks a million.'

'It looks a million dollars, Judy,' he replied, his voice ringing with pride and admiration. 'The whole landscape is a fine advertisement for you. Should bring you in a lot of work.'

Like the Fairway Tourist Centre, she thought with a twinge of irony. Her work was very good but without Mal's weight behind it, her work alone would not have won that job for her. And there would be other big jobs if she lived with

Mal. He would see that she was given every scope for her talent. He was not the kind of man who would begrudge her success. He not only loved her he believed in her talent and was proud of her work. Such a man was unlikely to cross her path again. Maybe he would even agree to having children. Maybe a marriage certificate was irrelevant, providing they loved each other enough.

Her father insisted on helping with the tidying up process of edging the kerb with turf. By three o'clock it was done and both of them stood at the entrance to the driveway and heaved sighs of satisfaction.

'Coming home now?'

She shook her head. 'I'll wait to see Mal. All the documentation is in the truck. I'd like to give it to him personally.'

'Uh-huh. Is he expecting to see you?' The question was cautious, the tone slightly strained.

'Yes,' she answered shortly, not looking at her father.

There was a short pause before he asked, 'What time should we expect you home?'

'I don't know, Dad,' she answered truthfully. 'Tell Mum . . . Tell Mum not to wait dinner for me.'

She had not been able to keep the strain of decision out of her voice and still she did not look at her father for fear of betraying her desperate uncertainty about the future.

A hand closed over her shoulder, squeezing it gently. She held her breath but no word came from her father. The heavy silence could not be borne.

'Yes?' Her voice wavered on the word. Judy

stared fixedly at the ground. Her foot moved to scrape flat a little mound of gravel.

'Just remember that your mother and I love you.' The assurance was poignant with sadness.

Tears blurred Judy's eyes. Her throat worked convulsively, gulping back a huge lump of emotion. It was impossible to speak.

Another light squeeze on her shoulder. 'I'll leave you to it then.'

His footsteps crunched heavily on the gravel as he walked away. The cabin door of the semi-loader opened and shut. The engine roared into life. Judy turned to watch it go, intensely grateful for her father's understanding, yet shamed by it. She had said nothing about Mal to her parents, denying them her confidence, but she now realised that both of them had sensed that today was a critical time for their daughter.

Judy did not want to hurt them. Billy would never marry. It was only natural that they would have looked forward to their daughter's marrying and providing them with grandchildren. She knew they would not stop loving her if she chose another life-style but her heart was torn with the choice being forced upon it.

She drove the truck up to the courtyard. With her folder of papers under one arm she strolled down the side-path, checking that the seedlings in the kitchen garden were thriving. She unlocked the laundry door, walked through to the kitchen and laid the folder on the kitchen bench. The house seemed very empty as if waiting for people to inject life into it and make it a home. Her home, if she said yes.

She opened the glass doors on to the back patio and stepped outside. Her gaze swept around, gleaning satisfaction from the results of her hard work. She could share all this with Mal, share the pleasure of seeing everything grow, shrubs coming into flower, leaves turning colour with the seasons. She only had to say yes.

Hello or goodbye. She did not know which to say to him. In a restless state of mind Judy did the rounds of the outside taps, turning them on so that the sprinklers would go to work. Watering was vital to a new landscape, particularly while roots were still establishing themselves. She was watching the spray gradually reach out to the new grass by the kerb when the Aston Martin turned into the driveway. Her heart gave a painful lurch. Then to her puzzlement another car turned in. Had Mal brought reinforcements to persuade her into taking the Fairway job?

The second car crawled forwards, its occupants more intent on looking than arriving. It suddenly stopped and to Judy's amazement, Ruth Hagan stepped out of the passenger side. The car moved on towards the courtyard and Ruth walked towards Judy, a delighted smile on her face and arms sweeping round to encompass the whole front area.

'Who would have thought you could turn such scrubby country into such a beautiful haven? Judy, I am simply astonished!'

Judy smiled. This was a woman with no affectations. Her pleasure was patently sincere. 'Hello, Ruth. I'm glad you like it.'

'Like it! I love it!' She linked her arm in Judy's and turned her towards the courtyard. 'Mal's been singing your praises and now I can certainly see why. You must give me a personal tour of the whole lot. I believe the back area is quite spectacular and the kitchen garden the envy of every housewife.' She cast Judy a sly glance. 'Which reminds me. Before we join the men, may I say how very glad I am that you won.'

'Won?' Judy frowned over the curious word. 'Ruth, I don't know what you're talking about.'

Ruth gave a soft laugh and squeezed Judy's hand. 'I wasn't sure if Mal's sleek armour of sophistication would crack open for you but it has. He is quite desperately in love with you. Don't you know that?'

Judy frowned even more heavily. Was Mal using Ruth as his advocate? Is that why he had asked the Hagans here this afternoon?

'Judy?' Ruth looked puzzled. 'You do love him, don't you? I wasn't mistaken that night at Vivien's?' She paused in her step and looked searchingly at the younger girl.

Judy gave her a wry little smile. 'No. You weren't mistaken, but love isn't all rosy dreams, is it?'

'No. No, it's not,' came the serious reply. 'But you value anything far more if you have to fight for it. It might seem that Patrick and I have never been in conflict, yet we both went through hell before we married. Love's worst enemy is pride. Remember that, Judy. I can't give you better advice.'

'Thanks, Ruth. You're very kind,' Judy muttered, a little comforted by the well-meant words, yet not quite sure if Ruth spoke from the heart or was pleading Mal's cause.

They turned into the gateway and came face to face with the men. Defensively Judy's gaze fastened on Patrick Hagan who proceeded to lavish compliments on her and her work. She could feel Mal's eyes boring into her but she did not feel ready to give him an answer. He invited his guests to walk down the side-path, held the gate open for them all, then fell into step beside Judy. He said nothing to her and his very silence seemed to emphasise the enormous gap still between them.

'I put the completed sketches and documentation on the island-bench in the kitchen,' she muttered to him and felt hot blood scorch into her cheeks with the effort at opening communication.

'Thank you.' A hesitation, then, 'Judy, you will stay for a while . . . please?'

She flicked a glance at him and her breath caught in her throat at the intense vulnerability in the green eyes. It suddenly struck her that he was in as much torment as she and instinctively her heart went out to him. He was afraid she would go and Judy knew intuitively that this was the reason he had invited the Hagans, not only to cover the awkwardness of meeting after last week's dreadful argument but to help build a bridge of communication.

'Yes, I'll stay,' she whispered and wrenched her gaze away.

So what if he wouldn't marry her! They'd still have each other, wouldn't they? And she wanted so much to be with him. Suddenly her hand was caught. Strong fingers threaded between hers and gripped tightly. She did not pull away. She wanted his hold, wanted to be held in his keeping forever.

They accompanied Ruth and Patrick on a tour of the whole grounds. Judy found it difficult to answer their interested questions. Her whole being was intensely concentrated on the man at her side. Eventually Mal fetched sun-loungers from the store-room in the cabana and set them on the patio. They sat there, watching the sun lower in the west and drinking long, cool drinks.

Most of the conversation came from the Hagans. Judy could not help noticing the wonderful understanding between them. Their eyes spoke to each other with the intimacy of joined hearts and minds. Judy envied that intimacy. It seemed so natural, completely without artifice or tension, and with absolutely no trace of doubt that it would always be theirs.

It was not until Ruth and Patrick began talking of their children that the knife of envy really twisted in Judy's heart. Their two sons were destructive little monsters where gardens were concerned, according to the amusing anecdotes told by both their parents, but it was perfectly obvious they were much-loved children.

Marriage. Family. The Hagans were a glowing example of how it could be. They had the reality of Judy's dreams, what she had always wanted more than anything else. More than a successful career. More than a love without commitment. Her heart might belong to Mal but even that love could never expel this deep yearning.

She knew now. She knew what she had to do. Slowly, harnessing every shred of will-power she possessed, Judy rose to her feet. She could not address Mal, could not risk weakening at this crucial moment.

'I hope you'll excuse me. I really must be going. It was nice to see you again, Ruth, Patrick.' She nodded to them and managed a stiff little smile.

Polite comments were made. Judy was barely conscious of them but she made automatic responses. There was a pain growing inside her which had to be contained, hidden until parting had been effected. Mal insisted that she go through the house to the courtyard and his grip on her elbow allowed no argument. A few minutes of his company. That's all she had to bear, Judy reasoned desperately.

His fingers tightened hurtfully as they crossed the living-room. 'Why are you going? Why?' he hissed at her.

'I have to.' Flat, toneless, dead words.

'But you will do the Fairway job,' he insisted urgently.

'No. I won't do it.'

'Judy, I swear to you it's nothing more than a job. I want you to have it.'

'I can't take it.'

'Why not?' It was a passionate entreaty.

They were at the front door. She reached out and opened it. For one moment she paused, looking up at him with agonised eyes. 'Because I'd see you there, Mal, and I can't stand any more. Goodbye.'

She ran from him then. He caught her before she could reach the truck, swinging her back into a fiercely possessive embrace.

'I love you. I won't let you go.'

He was breathing heavily and his eyes were ablaze with wild emotion. She shook her head in speechless grief.

'Judy, please. Say you love me. I know you do but say it. Say it,' he commanded.

Tears glazed her eyes. The words poured from a bursting dam of despair. 'I love you.'

'Then stay with me. Live with me,' he pleaded hoarsely.

'No—o—o.' The moan tore her throat and with another upsurge of pain came the deep cry from her heart. 'I want what they have. Go back and look at Ruth and Patrick. Marriage didn't corrupt their love, Mal. They've got it all. A family unit bonded with love and security. That's what I want and you'll never give it to me. So let me go. Let me go. You're tearing me apart and I can't take any more.'

His hold loosened and she broke away. He let her go. He was still standing in the same place when she reversed the truck ready to drive out of the courtyard. His face was pale as if stricken with shock. She had to steer around him and she took the image of sickened green eyes with her on the long journey away from him.

CHAPTER TEN

SHE parked the truck in the shed near the nursery and made a slow trek of the walk up to the house, formulating a number of necessary resolutions on the way. The job was behind her. Malcolm Stewart was behind her. Both of them had divorced her from her family over the last three weeks. It was time to rejoin the fold and be the daughter and sister she had always been. The future might look a deadly blank now but common sense told her it would take on shape as time passed. She had made her decision and it would serve no purpose to mourn for something that could not be.

Putting a brave, determined face on her inner misery, Judy entered the house and walked through to the kitchen. Her mother was at the stove. Her father was sitting at the kitchen table sipping a sherry. Billy was setting out cutlery for the evening meal.

'Set a place for me too please, Billy. I'm home for dinner after all, Mum,' she said in a fair attempt at nonchalance. 'Think I'll join you in a sherry, Dad. No, don't get up. I'll pour my own.' She swept an over-bright smile at all of them and headed for the cupboard where the sherry was kept.

Her father cleared his throat. 'Ah, Judy. Did you, by chance, invite Malcolm Stewart for dinner?'

She shot him a pained look. 'Of course not.'

His eyebrows lifted then drew together as he nodded towards the window. 'His car's just come through the gateway.'

Her head jerked around in time to see a flash of the Aston Martin before it disappeared from view. Her carefully fixed composure cracked and sheer anguish twisted across her face. 'No! No more!' Her eyes sought her father's in desperate plea. 'You've got to stop him, Dad. I can't see him. I can't! It's over. It's got to be over.'

'Judy!' her mother gasped in shock.

Billy's mouth gaped open.

Judy covered her face with her hands, mortified at having revealed such naked pain. A great shudder ran through her body. She was breaking up. The stress was too great. It was no good. No good. She couldn't face Mal again. Why, oh why had he followed her? Hadn't it all been said?

Her father wrapped comforting arms around her and pressed her sagging head against his chest, soothing her distress with the little pats he had always used whenever she had run to him with her hurts.

'Don't you worry, love. You don't have to see him,' he assured her softly. 'I'll send him away. You're sure that's what you want now.'

'Yes.' It was a harsh sob of despair.

A loud hammering at the front door demanded attention.

Her father urged Judy over to a chair and sat her down. 'Now you just calm yourself down. I'll handle this. Tess, pour Judy that glass of sherry.'

Her mother fluttered around anxiously, pushing a glass into Judy's hand and standing sentinel as her father moved away. The hammering on the door had not abated.

'I'll be back in a minute,' her father promised and went to confront the caller.

Her mother's hand slid around Judy's shoulders, a silent affirmation of love and support. Judy blinked back tears and flicked an apologetic look upwards. 'I'm sorry, Mum. I'm a mess.'

'Never mind, love. You need some looking after. That's all,' Tess Campbell murmured soothingly.

'I thought you liked Mal,' Billy remarked in puzzled fashion.

'Hush, Billy. Not now,' his mother cautioned.

The hammering stopped. The ensuing silence screeched on Judy's nerves. She held her breath.

'Mr Campbell . . .' Mal's voice, clearly audible, ringing with harsh urgency, '. . . I must see Judy.'

'If it's to do with business, Mr Stewart . . .' Calm, unhurried words, cut off in mid-sentence.

'No, no. Not business. It's a personal matter. Very personal.' Impatient. Harried.

'Then I'm sorry but Judy has no wish to see you.' Firm and unequivocal. 'You're not welcome here, Mr Stewart. Please go.' An emphatic dismissal.

Silence. Judy could hear her heart beating a painful dirge. Her gaze dropped wearily to the glass in her hand. It was shaking. She took a quick gulp of fortifying liquid.

'Mr Campbell . . .' Steely purpose in Mal's voice. ' Judy and I . . .'

'I'm not blind, Mr Stewart,' her father whipped in with equal steel. 'Nor am I blind to my daughter's distress. Please go.'

Another silence. More excruciating.

'No . . . No, I won't go.' Grim determination. 'I love your daughter, Mr Campbell, more deeply than I ever imagined loving anyone. And she feels the same way about me. I've come to ask Judy to marry me. And I demand the right to be heard.'

Marry! He wanted to propose marriage? The thought stunned Judy for a moment. But only for a moment. He was just saying that. It was only a ploy to get past her father. He couldn't mean it. Not after all he had said and done.

Her mother's hand gently squeezed her shoulder. Judy looked up into questioning eyes. She shook her head despondently and took another large sip of sherry, almost choking on it as she heard her father's next words.

'Well, if that's the case, you'd better come in, Mr Stewart, if for no other reason than I'd like to see your arrogance humbled.'

Oh God! No! Judy shot to her feet, looked wildly around her, then realising there would be no ultimate escape from this last confrontation she backed to the furthest end of the kitchen away from the door and leaned hard against the cupboards for support. The large blue eyes glittered with the feverish life of a hounded animal.

'Judy, for goodness sake! We're here. With you,' Tess Campbell expostulated in an attempt at reducing the tension, then swung on the two men, upbraiding them as they entered the kitchen. 'Drew! How could you? And you, Mr Stewart, haven't you done enough?'

It pulled them both up short. Tess Campbell was of small stature, but when aroused she was a formidable woman.

'My wife, Mr Stewart,' Drew Campbell said with almost a smug flourish in the introduction.

It was as if Mal had not heard a word of it. The green eyes locked on to Judy, pleading, demanding, insisting that she and only she existed for him. She gazed back, mesmerised by his need even while trying to harden her heart against him.

'Hello, Mal.' Billy's impulsive greeting broke the spell.

Making a visible effort to recover himself, Mal turned to address her brother. 'Hello, Billy.' He lifted his eyes to Judy's mother. 'Good evening, Mrs Stewart.' Polite but obviously distracted. His gaze returned to Judy, relentless in its quest. 'Will you come outside with me, Judy? I'd like to see you privately.'

'No!' She shook her head vehemently. No more would she be alone with him. She was far too vulnerable to give him such an advantage. 'Anything you want to say to me will have to be said in front of my family.' There! Let him try persuading her to live with him in the hearing of her parents and see how damned convincing he could be! The blue eyes blazed her challenge with unrelenting determination, pride and pain denying him any alternative.

He did not flinch from it. There was no wavering of purpose in his bearing or expression. He stared straight back at her, holding her gaze with even greater intensity. 'You think I mind declaring my love for you in front of your family?' he asked softly. He gave a slight shake of the head but his eyes maintained their hold on hers, insisting that she believe him. 'I don't mind. I'll declare it in front of the whole world.

Every day of our lives. We were meant for each other and you know it. Tomorrow I'm taking you to the closest registry office and we'll sign whatever papers have to be signed. I'm going to marry you and you're going to marry me as fast as it can be arranged.'

'You certainly will not!' Tess Campbell exploded indignantly. 'When my daughter gets married, Mr Stewart, she will be given a proper wedding in a church. Registry office indeed!'

The unexpected outburst distracted Mal, and Judy was grateful to her mother, not only for breaking Mal's hypnotic hold on her but for drawing attention to the weakness in his argument. A registry office dealt in paper and that was exactly how he viewed marriage. A piece of paper which he would not hesitate to tear up once it no longer served his purpose. He was only paying lip-service to her ideal.

'It's irrelevant to me where we're married, Mrs Stewart,' he was saying reasonably. 'In a church, if Judy wishes.'

'I like church weddings,' Billy chipped in eagerly. 'Lots and lots of flowers, and the organ playing . . .'

'Billy!' The stern silencer from Drew Campbell brought the tension back to full measure.

The green eyes sliced instantly to Judy, intent on burning away any resistance. 'Church, flowers, anything you want. Just name the day.' His mouth quirked into a little smile. 'We'll fly in the whole Welsh Choir if it'll make you feel more married.'

The smile did it. That and the Welsh Choir. All the agony of the last few hours erupted in bitter accusation. 'You'd say anything to get your own way, Malcolm Stewart. Anything at all!'

'Yes, I would,' he retorted sharply, fighting fire with fire. 'But it so happens that my way is your way this time, Judy. I want what you want. Or are you reneguing on the lifetime of loving you promised me?'

That was a hit below the belt. She sucked in a quick breath as a flush of confusion crept up her neck. 'You don't believe in marriage,' she threw at him defensively.

He bounced it right back at her. Forcefully. 'I believe in our marriage. We belong together. You know it. I know it. Stop fighting what we both want.'

She stared at him, doubts still searing her mind.

'Judy, do you want him to go?' Drew Campbell asked quietly.

She turned dazed eyes to her father. Slowly she shook her head.

'Would you like to be left alone with him?'

'I don't know,' she whispered. 'I don't know.' She reeled her gaze back to Mal, begging him for total sincerity.

He took a step towards her, hands outstretched in urgent appeal. Her heart pounded an insistent answer.

'Yes. Yes, I want to be alone with him,' she said jerkily. 'If . . . if you don't mind leaving us for a while.'

'We'll go and watch the news in the T.V. room,' her father said with pointed tact.

They slipped away. Judy did not really see them go. Mal was walking towards her and every nerve-end screeched at his nearness, wanting his touch but terrified of its power. She held up protesting hands to ward him off.

'No . . . please. We've got to talk.'

'What about?' He kept coming.

'You don't really want this,' she cried frantically.

'Yes, I do.'

'You'll regret it.'

'Never.' His hands were sliding around her waist.

Panic raced through her veins and she felt her heart would burst. 'You'll blame me for forcing you into it. You'll resent being tied down. You'll say . . . you'll say . . .'

Strong arms enfolded her trembling body and her voice was muffled in an embrace so possessive that she was lost to words anyhow. His hands relearnt the softness of her curves with almost worshipping fervour and his mouth brushed over her hair again again.

'I want you tied to me by every means possible, you impossible woman,' he said feelingly. 'No open ends. No loopholes for escape. You're mine and you're going to stay mine forever and a day. I'll sign a marriage contract every year of our lives if that's what's needed to keep you at my side. Willingly and gratefully. Because you're my woman, Judy, and I never want to lose you. I love you too deeply to ever let you go.'

'Oh, Mal,' she snuffled into his shirt as tears of relief gushed into her eyes. 'Hold me tight. I've been so . . . so bereft these last weeks.'

'Me, too,' he murmured huskily. 'Don't cry, my darling. There'll be no more torment between us.' He lifted her chin and gently kissed the tears from her cheeks.

She tried to smile. 'I wanted to give in today. I waited for you. I meant to stay . . .'

'I know. You don't have to explain, Judy.'

'But . . .'

'Sssh . . .' He put his finger up to her lips and his eyes were soft with understanding. 'It's all right. Truly.'

'I do love you, Mal. So much that I could hardly bear the hurt.'

His mouth tilted in a wry little smile. 'You weren't the only one working like a maniac, Judy. I was a blind, proud, stubborn fool to take the stance I did.'

'Oh, I was a fool, too. I'm terribly sorry for what I thought about Vivien, Mal. I was wretchedly jealous and . . .'

'Why are we talking?' he interrupted softly.

She slid her hands up around his neck and stood on tip-toe, eager to meet his kiss and give expression to all her long-suppressed feeling for him. Boundless relief, utter joy in their coming together, deep, deep gratitude for his determination and love . . . sweet, warm, beautiful love which outlasted all the rest, healing their hurts, filling them with blissful happiness and promising all manner of wonderful things for their future.

One kiss only served as an intoxicant, inspiring a compulsive urge for more and more satisfaction. Drugged with love and driven by their desire for each other, they lost all sense of time and place until a very loud clearing of the throat recalled them to a more mundane reality. Judy drew in a sharp, steadying breath and peered shyly over Mal's shoulder.

'Yes, Dad?'

He gave her a rueful grin. 'The news is over, it is seven o'clock, and your mother's worrying about the casserole burning. Would you mind turning off the oven if you wish to continue?'

Mal loosened their embrace and turned, hugging Judy possessively to his side. 'Don't go, Mr Campbell. I know it's somewhat late in the day and my manner, particularly this evening, must have seemed extremely arrogant, but I assure you it's a humble man who asks you now for your daughter's hand in marriage.'

The faint reserve which had remained on Drew Campbell's face throughout Mal's speech, suddenly melted into a smile. 'Mr Stewart, that was handsomely said, although perhaps irrelevent since I don't imagine Judy would allow me any say in the matter. However, I will admit to a grudging admiration for the way you conducted yourself this evening under ... shall we say ... difficult circumstances. I'm prepared to welcome you as my son-in-law.'

He walked forward and offered his hand which Mal shook with emphatic vigour.

'There is one thing though,' Drew Campbell drawled, and the twinkle in his eyes was definitely suspect.

'Name it,' said Mal, beaming with good will.

'I'll grant you the Welsh Choir is very good, but I always fancied bag-pipes playing "Amazing Grace" at Judy's wedding.'

'Bag-pipes!' Mal repeated incredulously.

'Grand stuff!' Drew rolled out with relish.

Mal started to laugh. 'Why not?' he spluttered and burst into peals of merriment.

Judy dug her elbow into his ribs. 'Dad's pulling your leg. He doesn't mean it, Mal.'

'Oh, but I mean it, Judy love,' Mal gurgled out, still shaking with laughter. 'If the Campbells won't come up with the bag-pipes, by God! the Stewarts will! I insist upon it.'

'Ah . . . a man after my own heart,' the head of the Campbells boomed with satisfaction. 'Call me Drew, my boy.'

'Mal.'

They shook hands again, huge grins on their faces.

'Better see to the casserole, Judy,' her father reminded her cheerfully. 'It's going to have to stretch to five people. Tess, Billy, you can come in now. The wedding's all settled.'

The wedding was not all settled. Tess Campbell was quite affronted by her husband's declaration. She had very fixed ideas on how a wedding should be run and proceeded to tell them so, after the first few awkward minutes of accepting Malcolm Stewart as Judy's husband-to-be. To Judy's astonishment and delight, Mal threw himself wholeheartedly behind the concept of a grand wedding. Having shed his prejudice against marriage, he became enthusiastically intent on planning a ceremony and celebration which would live in their memory all the days of their lives.

And it was. Church bedecked with flowers, everyone in formal dress, the organ making the church walls resound with the splendid grandeur of traditional music, not the Welsh Choir, but a sweet-voiced children's choir singing favourite hymns, and immediately after the solemn vows were exchanged, a lone piper in full ceremonial dress piping the haunting beauty of 'Amazing Grace'.

It was a wonderful day, a day bubbling with happiness, a day of smiles which showered the joyful couple with warm-hearted approval, a day of eloquent speeches and much laughter and sentimental tears, but most of all a day of love, publicly declared and privately expressed with the special tenderness that only a wedding day inspires, the total giving to each other with the awesome realisation that this is the real beginning and now is forever.

As the day ticked away its last minutes, Judy and Mal lay entwined, blissfully content and tired with the happy fatigue which comes when all has been done to total satisfaction. For a long time only their soft breathing had whispered across the silence. Mal's sudden chuckle startled Judy.

'What's amusing you?' she asked, hitching herself up to smile down at him.

His grin was one of mischievous delight. 'I was just planning what I'd say to our future son-in-law when he comes proposing to our eldest daughter.'

'He might not come proposing,' she teased.

'Oh, yes he will. Any daughter of ours will make him toe the line.'

Judy laughed then slowly sobered. 'Mal, you don't regret it, do you? Having to marry me?'

His hands came up and tenderly cupped her face and his eyes glowed up at her with a love which held no shade of doubt. 'Judy, this has been the happiest day of my life and only you could have made it possible. How could I regret anything ...' he smiled, '... you wonderful, impossible woman.'

And he kissed any such ridiculous thoughts right out of her mind.

Best Seller Romances

Romances you have loved

Each month, Mills & Boon publish three Best Seller Romances. These are the love stories that have proved particularly popular with our readers – they really are 'back by popular demand'. All give you the chance to meet fascinating people. Many are set in exotic faraway places.

If you missed them first time around, or if you'd like them as presents for your friends, look out for Mills & Boon Best Sellers as they are published. And be sure of the very best stories in the world of romance.

On sale where you buy paperbacks. If you have any difficulty obtaining them write to: Mills & Boon Reader Service, P.O. Box 236, Thornton Rd, Croydon, Surrey CR9 3RU, England. Readers in South Africa – please write to Mills & Boon Reader Service of Southern Africa, Private Bag X3010, Randburg 2125, S. Africa.

Mills & Boon
the rose of romance

Take 4
Exciting Books
Absolutely
FREE

Love, romance, intrigue... all are captured for you by Mills & Boon's top-selling authors. By becoming a regular reader of Mills & Boon's Romances you can enjoy 6 superb new titles every month plus a whole range of special benefits: your very own personal membership card, a free monthly newsletter packed with recipes, competitions, exclusive book offers and a monthly guide to the stars, plus extra bargain offers and big cash savings.

AND an Introductory FREE GIFT for YOU.
Turn over the page for details.

As a special introduction we will send you four exciting Mills & Boon Romances Free and without obligation when you complete and return this coupon.

At the same time we will reserve a subscription to Mills & Boon Reader Service for you. Every month, you will receive 6 of the very latest novels by leading Romantic Fiction authors, delivered direct to your door. You don't pay extra for delivery — postage and packing is always completely Free. There is no obligation or commitment — you can cancel your subscription at any time.

You have nothing to lose and a whole world of romance to gain.

Just fill in and post the coupon today to **MILLS & BOON READER SERVICE, FREEPOST, P.O. BOX 236, CROYDON, SURREY CR9 9EL.**

Please Note:- READERS IN SOUTH AFRICA write to Mills & Boon, Postbag X3010, Randburg 2125, S. Africa.